WAR TRAIN

BY DONALD WILLERTON

WAR TRAIN

A MOGI FRANKLIN MYSTERY
BOOK 10

DONALD WILLERTON

WISE WOLF
BOOKS

War Train
Paperback Edition
Copyright © 2025 (As Revised) by Donald Willerton

Wise Wolf Books
An imprint of Wolfpack Publishing
1707 E. Diana Street
Tampa, FL 33610

wisewolfbooks.com

This book is a work of fiction. Any references to historical events, real people or real places are used fictitiously. Other names, characters, places and events are products of the author's imagination, and any resemblance to actual events, places or persons, living or dead, is entirely coincidental.

Paperback ISBN 978-1-965596-25-8
Ebook ISBN 978-1-965596-24-1

For My Mother

WAR TRAIN

CHAPTER 1

OCTOBER 16, 1943, LAS VEGAS, NEW MEXICO

A cool breeze swept down the street along the railroad tracks, and an early winter chill bit the autumn air.

October was an especially pretty time of year in New Mexico, and the small park across from the Las Vegas State Bank gave the cottonwoods a stage for showing off their beauty to anyone who would take the time to sit and enjoy it.

Harold Lennon glanced out the bank windows and saw a flurry of dry leaves caught in a swirling gust of wind. It convinced him to eat lunch at his desk rather than his usual bench in the park. He would miss the beauty of the trees' splendid colors, but staying inside would keep the blowing dirt from peppering his sandwich.

Harold would also miss his time alone. Sitting on

the bench was his daily escape from helping scurrying clerks, serving confused customers, and attending to his meticulous ledgers. Spending time in the park and briefly forgetting his duties as the bank's senior clerk allowed him to relax and watch the trains come and go from the depot. The sheer power of the massive machines, the hissing of the steam, and the deep rhythm of their noise made him think of a chorus of great metal beasts singing on the tracks.

He especially liked watching the hustle and bustle of the troop trains. It had been almost two years since the Japanese attack on Pearl Harbor had suddenly plunged the United States into what the government called a *mobilization for war* that had touched every corner of America. In 1939, the United States Army ranked thirty-ninth in the world in terms of military strength, possessing a cavalry force of fifty thousand men who still used horses to pull artillery. It had no air force, and what the Army Air Corps did have still included an assortment of decades-old biplanes. Add to that the Navy's losing a significant part of its fleet in the attack in Hawaii and it was obvious that it would be a while before America could become ready to fight the already-sophisticated and well-equipped German and Japanese militaries.

First and foremost, putting together an armed fighting force meant millions of men and women joining the effort. Needing to build an army, navy, air corps, merchant marine, and coast guard of battle-ready soldiers, sailors, pilots, submariners, doctors, nurses, secretaries, officers, technicians, and support personnel meant incredible recruitment and training programs all across the continent. And it meant building the industrial capacity to supply that military force.

Since the government relied on trains to transport recruits to hundreds of training camps, academies, bases, harbors, and airfields, Harold had grown used to seeing troop trains speed through the town. He had seen hundreds of them, and with Las Vegas on one of the major routes connecting the western half of the US to the eastern half, the depot was a constant hotspot of military activity. Troop trains appeared and disappeared at irregular times every day.

As he sat at his desk, Harold heard a locomotive's in-coming whistle and imagined the young men in their khaki uniforms, hundreds of them spilling out of the cars, running across the wide platform and down the sidewalk to the eatery, starving from their long ride, muscles stiff and ready to be free of the hard seats they had been crammed into, talking, laughing, releasing their pent-up energy. They would soon be crowding through the doors of the Fred Harvey diner and restaurant on the first floor of the Castañeda Hotel, anxious to spend time with the pretty waitresses and already planning which pie or cake to order with their meals.

A few minutes later, Harold glanced up from his columns of numbers as two men came into the bank.

The first thing he noticed was how they were dressed.

While the usual attire of men from the largely

rural Las Vegas area included loose-hanging, faded cotton shirts, worn overalls, rough work boots, and sweat-stained fedoras, these men wore new blue denim overalls, still-creased long-sleeved shirts buttoned to the neck, and clean wide-brimmed hats pulled down over their foreheads. Their shoes were polished to a gleam that he could see across the room.

Harold's attention then moved from the men's out-of-place appearance to the pistols held in front of them. He watched as the guns brought gasps and cries from the customers and employees. One of the two men hushed the small uproar and calmly told everyone to move to the back of the room. As they obeyed, he took a silver pocket watch from his overalls, checked the time, and nodded to his partner.

The other man, who had already disarmed the bank's guard, commanded him to lock the front door then added himself to the crowd. He walked the length of the three teller windows to the railing separating the tellers from the clerks' desks. He stood pointing his pistol at Harold's face, whose frozen expression had yet to change from surprise to fear.

The man used the tip of his pistol barrel to direct Harold into the open walk-in vault. He pulled a large green cotton bag from the side opening of his overalls, threw it to Harold, and held the pistol steady as Harold stepped quickly to a large sorting table next to the back wall.

Harold, who had yet to utter a word, needed no instructions. He was soon sliding thick stacks of hundred-dollar bills off the table into the bag.

The stacked bills on the table had arrived early that morning by train from a federal repository bank in Kansas City. Taken out of their secure strongboxes and laid out in neat rows, the bills were set to be counted, sorted, and placed into large, lockable bank bags that would be distributed to the railroad offices, hotels, government offices, and other businesses in town. The bandits' efficiency and apparent knowledge of the bank's operations made clear to Harold that the robbery had been well-planned.

The man pointing a gun at him switched it to his other hand, pulled his own silver watch from the top pocket of his overalls, and glared intensely at its face. Glancing from Harold to the watch, then from the watch to Harold, his head began nodding in time. A minute later, he told the senior clerk to tie the bag closed and throw it out the vault door.

Evidently, that was the signal for the other gunman to herd the customers and employees into the vault with Harold, who moved to the back to give them more room. When the last person had passed through, the heavy door was closed and the handle spun. Voices of relief filled the vault as Harold pressed the silent alarm button hidden behind a cabinet door.

But it didn't take long for them to notice that there was no ventilation. People felt the lack of fresh air, started to sweat, and began milling around, muttering that it would soon be hard to breathe. Harold assured them the alarm button had been pushed, police were probably already outside, and everyone should resist the urge to panic.

Fifteen minutes later, a police officer banged on the vault door and yelled for them to be patient until the door could be opened. The bank president was being sought for the combination.

When the door was finally unlocked and pulled back, Harold and the others walked out into fresh air and freedom. As the rattled employees and customers gave their statements to the police, more officers and state troopers rushed about the bank, marking off various areas, searching for clues, and dusting for fingerprints. Outside, several screaming police cars had come and gone, the area around the bank was blocked off, officers were searching nearby cars and buildings, and roadblocks were set up on the highways. The full force of local and state police was brought into action to find and capture the thieves.

But as many searchers as there were, as long as they worked, and as hard as they looked, no trace whatsoever was ever found of the two men.

The bank robbers had simply vanished.

CHAPTER 2

PRESENT DAY

From: JenFranklin17@excellqx.net   Thursday, 9:12 p.m.

 To: MogiFranklin&1@excellqx.net

I can't believe it!!! It's the end of June, I've worked so hard and there's so much to do, and now they've dumped some silly PR work on me!!! I've worked my butt off to keep up with the class-work and reading assignments, and now I'm supposed to ride herd on a bunch of old ladies??? This is not what a summer intern should be doing and I'm going to complain!!!!!!!!!!!!!

From: MogiFranklin&1@excellqx.net   Thursday, 9:14 p.m.

 To: JenFranklin17@excellqx.net

Whoa! Any more exclamation points and your router will blow up. I need more information.

From: JenFranklin17@excellqx.net Thursday, 9:16 p.m.

To: MogiFranklin&1@excellqx.net

Sorry. You remember the program I'm in, right? High school intern for the architecture department at Highlands U. in Las Vegas, working on an architectural assessment of an old hotel?

The hotel, called the Castañeda, was built in 1898 by the railroad as a stopover for train passengers. It was a famous Harvey House. Fred Harvey was the guy who built restaurants all over the Southwest so people could get decent food when they traveled by train. The hotel looks like a huge Spanish hacienda, but it went out of business after World War II when travel by train dropped off in favor of buses and cars. It's been abandoned for years, and it's absolutely spooky.

Some guy bought it last year. He's restoring parts of the building to have restaurants, shops, and rentable hotel rooms. The rest will be high-end condos. He's going to open the hotel this summer and invite the townspeople in to show his progress and what it will look like when it's finished. I expect he'll try to get a jump on selling the condos too.

Well, now he has the bright idea to use the

open house to host a reunion for the women who worked as waitresses back when the original restaurant was still in business.

They were called Harvey Girls, after their famous boss. And my teacher drafted me to do the invitations and manage the party!!! That's not what I want!!! I want to do ARCHITECTURE stuff, not manage a bunch of old women!!!

From: MogiFranklin&1@excellqx.net   Thursday, 9:20 p.m.

To: JenFranklin17@excellqx.net

Come on, tell me how you really feel! You're responsible for a reunion, huh? Better get a more positive attitude toward those old women—you'll be one too someday, ya know. Have I mentioned that you're getting wrinkles and your butt's getting kind of saggy? Besides, whatever you've got going on, it's better than being a summer stock boy at the Bluff Trading Post here in hot and dusty Utah.

You know how many boxes of Pop-Tarts they sell? Good grief! And you wouldn't believe how many cases of beer I put out over a weekend. Beer and Pop-Tarts—no wonder the country's so overweight.

From: JenFranklin17@excellqx.net   Thursday, 9:32 p.m.

To: MogiFranklin&1@excellqx.net

Okay, you have it worse than me and I'll stop ranting. I like architecture—getting involved in the design of buildings, how they're built, how they operate—that sort of stuff.

Seeing the Castañeda being taken down to the bare bones is flat-out fascinating to me. I go to class three days a week, learn all sorts of history related to designing and building things, then work two days in the hotel.

My team is going through the building ahead of the demolition crew, collecting samples of materials that might be original to when the hotel was built. We look for carpet, wallpaper, paint, trim pieces, stained glass, furniture, bathroom fixtures, lights, and other stuff, and then we tuck it away in a room on the second floor. It's like a mini-museum. We photograph everything we find and stick the photographs in a binder. We'll write a report at the end of the summer, telling how the hotel was designed and built, where the furniture and materials came from, and all that.

The owner will get our mini-museum of stuff and I don't know who will get the report and the binder. One of the university's architecture majors, Sue, is helping us.

I love doing this. They even found a hidden room that nobody knew existed. The demolition guys pulled the stucco off the walls of a small stairway that leads up to the belfry—that's a bell tower, except it never had a bell—and found a door that opened to a space under the roof.

Everybody on the team got to go in and look around. It was really cramped and dirty, with a thick coating of bat poop and loose insulation on the floor. It had lots of old bed frames that were unbelievably small, chairs, cots, dressers, mattresses, and old metal footlockers. We're going to take everything to an empty room, clean it up, take pictures, and then take it out to big storage trailers in the parking lot. The owner will sell whatever he can to antique dealers and museums and then give the rest away. I'll get to help if I don't get stuck writing banquet invitations for dozens of old women!!!!!!!

Sorry about the stockroom job. You're really good at organizing stuff, so I bet they'll name you Stockroom Boy of the Year! Maybe you'll find that stockroom management is your calling in life!!!

And my butt is NOT getting saggy!!!

From: MogiFranklin&1@excellqx.net   Thursday, 10:03 p.m.
To: JenFranklin17@excellqx.net
Is there a Nobel Prize for Stockroomism?
Wish I was there. It sounds like fun.

From: JenFranklin17@excellqx.net   Tuesday, 6:17 p.m.

To: MogiFranklin&1@excellqx.net

Oh, wonderful, now I get to do databases. I hate computer work!!! I have to find everybody who worked at the hotel before 1948, when the Castañeda closed. I'm supposed to contact the Fred Harvey Company historian, get the master list of all the Harvey Girls, find out who's still alive, and mail everyone invitations. Fred Harvey was famous for hiring young, attractive, single women, typically from big cities back East. There weren't many women in the Southwest in the early 1900s, and every unmarried man for miles around made it a point to eat at the Harvey Houses so they could meet the waitresses. Anyway, lots of marriages means lots of name changes, so how am I supposed to handle that??? It's been more than a hundred years!!! It's going to take a ton of work.

I'm sunk!!!

From: MogiFranklin&1@excellqx.net   Tuesday, 6:20 p.m.

To: JenFranklin17@excellqx.net

Have I got a deal for you. Remember Howard Atticy? He's looking for a job for the rest of the summer and was asking me if they needed another stock boy at the trading post. They don't, but it gave me an idea. Your internship is like you're taking a class, right? With room and board thrown in?

How about this: I'll get Howard to take over for me in July and August, you get your teacher to make me a non-official part of the team, and she gets the university to give me a dorm room for free. I'll do all the database work—Harvey Girls, railroad stuff, any research you need. I'll make the past employee list, create the invitations, send them out, manage the responses, and even make posters for the open house. Howzat? I'm good at this stuff, I won't get in the way of your social life, and I promise to take a shower at least once a week.

From: JenFranklin17@excellqx.net   Tuesday, 7:00 p.m.

To: MogiFranklin&1@excellqx.net

I hate to deprive you of a chance at the Nobel Prize in Stockroomism, but I would love it if you'd help!!! I want to get into the architecture stuff, not be the Old Lady Luncheon organizer. I'll talk to Dr. Sanford, the professor who's teaching the class and leading the assessment team, and I'll get back to you. If this works, I'll come home next weekend and get you.

From: MogiFranklin&1@excellqx.net   Tuesday, 9:12 p.m.

To: JenFranklin17@excellqx.net

Woohoo!!!!!

From: JenFranklin17@excellqx.net   Tuesday, 9:30 p.m.

To: MogiFranklin&1@excelqx.net

By the way, remember that I told you about the crew finding a hidden attic that had a ton of junk squirreled away? Well, one of the footlockers had a padlock on it and was full of stuff!!! The team cut the lock off and we found a quilt, a shoebox full of bills and papers, a leather-covered Bible, some clothes, a bunch of old newspapers, a bundle of letters, and two really nice silver pocket watches with silver chains and everything. We wound them up and they still work! The newspapers date from 1943, which was in the middle of World War II, so the stuff has been locked away for more than seventy-five years!!!!

Who would leave all their stuff behind? And why? I doubt anything is worth much, but it's definitely a mystery. You'll have something to keep you busy while you're here!

CHAPTER 3

"I think it's haunted," Sue said.

"All old hotels are haunted," Jennifer replied.

"No, really." Sue had the dorm room next to Jennifer's. She was a senior at Highlands and was serving as an assistant to the Summer Intern Architecture Program.

"When my sister was in school here, she said students would sneak into the Castañeda to drink beer and mess around. She said there were always eerie things going on inside, like noises and screams and crying and stuff."

"My kind of place," Mogi said with a smile. "Does it still happen? Did they see any ghosts? Do you think we'll see one?"

It was the first Monday of July. Everything had worked out for Howard Atticy to take over for the rest of the summer, which made Mogi's parents happy that he'd have a better work experience than stocking shelves with Pop-Tarts and beer. Jennifer made a quick trip to Bluff, and her brother was now installed in the same co-ed dorm as she and Sue.

Sue smiled. "I'm not much into parties, so I haven't really checked it out, but I don't think we'll see any ghosts. When the place was sold to the new owner two years ago, they put up a fence and changed all the locks. Not that it made any difference to the ghosts, but it did stop the trespassing, so there aren't any eyewitnesses around anymore. But from what my sister said, I'm willing to believe there's some kind of spirit still haunting the place. I just doubt that it will show up for us."

Mogi Franklin was only fourteen but taller than either Jennifer or Sue, making him blend in with the older members of the Highlands team. His muscles had not yet caught up with his bones, so he was gangly and spindly and more than a little awkward. Mogi took after his mom in being shy and intro-verted, but he was the sum of both sides of the family for brain activity—he was usually way smarter than the people around him. He was quick-thinking and mentally disciplined, with a natural talent for solving puzzles, and his memory was extraordinary. He also loved messing around with computers, especially databases, treating the information as possible clues to still-undiscovered mysteries.

At seventeen, his sister, Jennifer, took after their father. Shorter than Mogi by several inches, with thick brown hair cut short, she was athletic and graceful. She loved being around people and had a keen sense of human nature. Whereas Mogi was the obsessively analytical, risk-taking problem-solver, Jennifer was the cautious, emotionally centered people person. It was no surprise that she found the architecture and contents of the Castañeda to be a rich reflection of the people who had lived and worked there.

The three signed in at the construction manager's trailer parked next to the hotel, put on their safety equipment, passed through a gate in the chain-link fence, and walked on in through the front door.

"You're sure you don't want to see the building first?" Sue asked.

"Absolutely not!" Mogi replied. "I want to see the footlocker! The footlocker! The footlocker! Lead me to the Awesome Mystery of the Castañeda Hotel!"

"Your brother is kind of super-focused, huh?" Sue said quietly to Jennifer.

"You have no idea," Jennifer replied, rolling her eyes.

"I should never have told him about the footlocker before he got here."

After going up the well-worn and creaky stairway, the three reached the assessment team's room. Sue, who had duplicate keys for some of the building's locks, opened the padlock and then the door.

Mogi didn't wait to be invited. He charged into the room.

"Ohboyohboyohboyohboy," he said with a grin, walking directly to the dusty green metal locker sitting on the floor beside a rusty bedframe and a horribly stained mattress.

"So, this is it. Did you take everything out and look at it?" he asked as he looked around the outside of the box.

"We photographed each individual item except for the pay stubs—we left them in the shoebox and photographed them all together. We also took pictures of the inside of the footlocker, as well as the outside, and then put everything back in."

Jennifer looked at Sue and shrugged. "It was interesting, but it's pretty common stuff. There's an old quilt, some clothing—"

"Don't tell me, don't tell me!" Mogi cried. "I want to see everything as if I've discovered it for the first time."

Jennifer pursed her lips, rolled her eyes at Sue, and said, "We'd better sit down. It will take a while for Sherlock here to get past himself."

Mogi knelt in front of the locker, carefully lifted the lid, and leaned it back against the bedframe.

One by one, he took each item from the locker and set it on the old mattress. Remembering what Jennifer had told him in her emails, he mentally ticked off the items as he handled them:

- The Bible, with its carved leather jacket,
- A shoebox with paycheck stubs and a few receipts from local stores,
- A stack of folded newspapers,
- Two heavily tarnished silver pocket watches, each with a silver chain attached,

- Various articles of clothing, including a lady's felt hat, a pair of worn black shoes, and three handkerchiefs,
- A set of sheets with two pillowcases,
- A large, lumpy quilt.

When the locker was empty, Mogi looked into each corner, down the sides, and inside the lid. "Do we know who the footlocker belonged to?" he asked.

"We do know, but let me give you some background," Sue said as she leaned forward in her chair. "I'm a double major in history and architecture, so Dr. Sanford asked me to handle the historical research on the hotel. When the footlocker was found, I looked everywhere to find where it came from and who it belonged to.

"There were a couple dozen Harvey Girls working here during the war years, from 1941 to 1945. That was twice the number as usual because the railroads were the biggest personnel and freight carriers in America, and they were doing far more traffic than ever before. Thousands of people were going through train stations all over the US, so every Harvey House was slammed with customers. The Harvey Company was constantly hiring women to work in their restaurants.

"Here at the Castañeda, they also had a *senior girl* who supervised everything. She made the daily schedule, managed the girls' time off, kept the service crisp and responsive in both dining rooms, and made sure that all the work was done to the quality standards that Fred Harvey expected.

"And, as if that weren't enough, the senior girl also served as house mother for the girls. They all lived together in a shared-room dormitory separate from the hotel, although the senior girl had her own room."

"Good grief," Mogi said. "I have trouble managing one sister."

Jennifer lit up like a rocket. "Managing? MANAG-ING? I think maybe you should reconsider your choice of words."

"Okay, you two can work this out later," Sue said. "Let's get back to the footlocker.

"A woman named Margaret Simpson was the senior girl at the Castañeda from 1935 to 1945. It's her name that's on the pay stubs in the footlocker. She must have left sometime after April of 1945, and since she didn't take her stuff, I guess she left in a hurry. That was around the end of the war in Europe, so maybe she quit to join someone who was coming back home."

"But she left a lot of stuff, including her Bible," Jennifer interjected. "Why would she do that?"

"Who knows? Maybe she couldn't take everything with her, or maybe she didn't want the memories. After so many years of war, maybe she just wanted to walk away."

"So everything belonged to Senior Girl Margaret Simpson," Mogi said, running his eyes over the contents laid out on the mattress. "I wonder why she had two watches?"

Taking a deep breath, he began to examine each item, starting with the quilt. He stood up and spread it out, barely holding the bottom off the floor. "This is the ugliest quilt I've ever seen," he said, folding it and placing it in the locker, covering the bottom.

He looked through the stack of newspapers, opening each one and scanning each page. The information seemed so ordinary. "I wonder what she found worth keeping in these papers," he said.

"There's a lot of war news," Jennifer said. "And local stuff. A lot of it is repetitive, like daily cartoons, the almanac forecast for the day, advertising, a social column with obituaries, weddings—things like that."

Mogi noticed that the seven newspapers were only from October 17, 1943, to November 9, 1943. Why was that three-week period important? What was happening with the war? Were the papers kept because they recorded something local or something national?

He refolded them and set them on top of the quilt, then did the same with the sheets, pillowcases, hat, shoes, and handkerchiefs, all seemingly unremarkable.

The shoebox was next. He took the top off and saw that the pay stubs had been stuffed in haphazardly, almost filling the box. The store receipts were tucked in at one side.

That will never do, Mogi thought, and dumped the contents on the mattress. Taking the pay stubs in groups, he sorted, stacked, and aligned them into piles, placing them back in the shoebox in date order.

It took several minutes, but he finished with ordered rows of stubs that fit exactly two across in the shoebox. Next, he read each of the store receipts, found nothing extraordinary, and then added them to the box. He fit the top back on and placed it in the footlocker.

Sue and Jennifer were slumped in their chairs, exhausted with boredom.

The two watches were interesting. Identical, with engraving around the case but no inscriptions inside or on the back. They looked to be good quality, and the tarnishing confirmed that they were made of real silver. Mogi wound both of them, and they were ticking away as he laid them on top of the handkerchiefs. Why two watches?

The last item was Margaret Simpson's Bible. It was about two inches thick, a King James version, and had no torn or loose pages, although there were pencil notations on almost every page. It was well-used and had been kept in good condition by the heavy leather cover that was beautifully carved, front and back, with intricate leather lacing around the edges. The book felt very personal, making it even more surprising that she would not have taken it. Why would Margaret Simpson leave her Bible behind?

After placing the Bible back in the footlocker, Mogi lowered the lid and latched it. He was disappointed, he had found nothing unusual.

It wasn't the startling mystery he'd expected. Except for the watches and the ugly quilt, nothing looked out of the ordinary.

"Wait a minute," he said, closing his eyes. A moment later, he opened them and looked at Jennifer. "Letters. Didn't you say there were letters or something?"

"Oh, yeah," she said, "fourteen small letters tied in a bundle with a ribbon, all written to Margaret Simpson. The history department borrowed them right after the footlocker was found. None of the letters were in envelopes, and they were all from the same soldier. I felt like I was spying on her, so I didn't read them."

"The professors in the history department almost fell out of their chairs when they heard what we'd found and couldn't wait to get their hands on them," Sue said.

"Finding original letters from soldiers during the war is a big deal."

"What are they going to do with them?" Mogi asked.

"They're photographing each one and will post the images on a website. Like I said, a big deal. I assume we'll get the letters back when they're done."

"Well, okay then," Mogi said as he straightened up, "Can I have a grand tour of the hotel now?"

CHAPTER 4

The Castañeda Hotel occupied an entire city block. It was a commanding two-story building with all the guest bedrooms and shared bathrooms upstairs while the downstairs held the lobby, a formal dining room, the lunchroom—in its heyday, the curving counter was more than sixty feet long, with pedestal seats—a bar, a cloak room, a humongous kitchen, a bakery, offices, workers' quarters, and storage rooms.

The U-shaped structure had a wide middle and two long wings extending around an interior courtyard, with all the exterior walls covered in rustic red brick. The first story surrounded by a deep porch, with brick arches supporting a roof of overlapping red clay tiles. The second story featured a line of guest room windows, each opening topped with a brick arch that mirrored the arches of the porch below.

The expansive roof over the building's three

sections was steeply pitched and covered with the same red tiles as below. In the center of the middle section was a wooden cupola. Long runs of dark green ivy grew up and around the arches of the porch, though what used to be a rich lawn circling the building was now patches of yellowed grass and weeds. A tall, circular, intricately carved stone fountain stood in the center of the courtyard, which opened eastward toward the railroad tracks. On the opposite side of the hotel, toward the mountains west of the city, was a long concrete sidewalk that ran alongside a row of tall, thick cottonwood trees bordering the street.

Its huge, ornately crowned, arched entryways resembled those of the traditional churches of Spain. Combined with the slanted tile roof, the hotel and its grounds looked like a huge hacienda from old Mexico. But it was a hacienda whose glory days were long past.

The hotel had cracks in its brick walls, rotting porch floors, peeling paint, and missing roof tiles. The surrounding grounds were pockmarked with gopher holes, bare patches of dirt, and a spiderweb of roots that had taken over the courtyard, spawning several scraggly trees that blocked the symmetry of the bricked archways.

Some windows were crooked, with panes shattered and sills broken or rotted. The ornate water fountain had probably been dry for half a century.

The hotel seemed to be squatting rather than standing regally, making it both imposing and spooky, as Jennifer had said. If the inside were as rundown as the outside, it would be an ideal residence for any number of ghosts and goblins. At night —with a full moon, the wind howling, owls hooting, and dogs barking in the distance—it could be the setting of a Stephen King novel. The building wasn't a ruin, but it had a heavy layer of history draped over it, weighing it down and cloaking it like a dark past.

Still, as Mogi looked it over, he couldn't help but be impressed. Even in its state of neglect, the architecture spoke of a rich Spanish ancestry, with outbuildings for Andalusian horses, carriages, a blacksmith's shop, granaries, and small houses for the peons working the land. One could imagine Zorro running across its roof.

Next door, a hundred yards south of the hotel, the train depot was a much smaller building. It had been designed with similar Spanish archways and red clay roof tiles, all well-maintained because it continued to serve as a working depot. The area between the depot and the tracks was a bricked landing that allowed substantial room for passengers, luggage, and freight. When the railroad business was booming, several trains a day pulled into the depot and let out hundreds of passengers, all finding the long sidewalk that led to the Castañeda's dining rooms.

The hotel's Harvey Girls were fast and professional as they poured gallons of fresh coffee and served plates of gravy-covered roast beef with peas, sugar-glazed chicken with asparagus, and large portions of meatloaf with oven-fried potatoes. The Harvey Houses were also famous for their large portions of high-quality baked goods: breads, rolls, cakes, pies, and other pastries that the diners chose from tall, glass-fronted cupboards behind the counter.

When finished, the fully satisfied passengers would hurry back to their train while the eatery's counter and seats were wiped down, silverware was washed and polished, plates were cleaned and restacked in rolling carts, cups were set on the tables, and more pies and cakes were sliced for the next rush of customers from the next train.

The more formal dining room tables also had their tablecloths replaced and bright white cloth napkins folded and set, ready for the next guests.

"That's the belfry I told you about," Jennifer said to Mogi as they stood in the courtyard between the two wings. She was pointing to the Spanish-styled cupola on the roof of the middle section.

"Right below it is where they uncovered the door to the attic," Sue added.

"So that's where the footlocker was found," Mogi said.

"I'm sorry it didn't have more treasure."

They continued walking around the end of the north wing. Other than the building's size, there was not as much to be impressed with here. The outside wall of the wing was a long run of two-story brick with no archways, no porch, and no entryways. It had guest room windows high on the second floor, while the first floor had only a few windows and three doors.

Mogi looked beyond the yard, a hundred yards north of the hotel, and saw a large, windowless building that was similarly bricked.

"Is that part of the hotel?" he asked.

"That's the steam building," Jennifer said. "It runs steam pipes underground to heat both the hotel and the train depot. It saved the builders a lot of money, not having to heat the buildings individually."

The three doors of the north wing were grouped together. One was an ordinary metal entry, next to it was a roller-type garage door opening onto a concrete pad, on the far side was an in-ground basement door, slanted from just above the grass to a metal ledge a couple of feet higher on the wall.

"That's the back door," Sue said as she pointed to the entry. "The roll-up door is for deliveries. Supplies brought by trains would be carted around and taken inside to the storerooms, the freezers, the bakery, which is the room on the corner, and the kitchen. Inside is a door that takes you down to the basement. I have a key for it, but after being given an introductory tour by the owner, it's strictly off-limits to us.

"The slanted door is a metal hatch that swings up and exposes a set of steps into the basement. That's what they use to swap out pipes and conduits. It has no handle or lock on the outside, you have to be in the basement to open it. Unfortunately, they found asbestos problems with some of the pipe insulation, so they welded a bar across the door until they can bring in a special contractor to remove it."

The three turned back, circled around the north wing, and walked across the courtyard. They stepped onto the porch and went through the hotel's rear entrance, finding themselves in the not-yet-demolished lunchroom, which took them into the front lobby.

The massive oak front desk and counter that served for a hundred-plus years as the hub of the hotel took up a full wall of the room. It had been refinished and polished to an impressive shine.

"The Castañeda," Sue said, "was finished by 1898 and was immediately successful, as was everything connected to the railroad at the beginning of the twentieth century. That lasted three decades, and then the hotel struggled during the Great Depression, like everything else, and almost closed. When World War II came along, the Fred Harvey hotels and restaurants —there were eighty at the time from Chicago to Los Angeles, down to Houston and up to San Francisco— came roaring back.

"In addition to passengers on regular trains, the military moved a lot of soldiers using *troop trains*, which were locomotives pulling dozens of passenger cars full of soldiers moving among military camps and bases. The soldiers had to eat, so the military made special arrangements with the restaurants along the routes. They crammed the soldiers into eating areas where the Harvey Girls dished out food like a factory. The men would wolf their food down in minutes, give their seats to the next soldiers, who would do the same, and then jump back on the train and take off. The two dining areas sometimes fed up to two thousand soldiers at one food break, and the government paid the bill.

"Look at this," Sue continued, pointing at a framed picture on the wall. "This is what the Harvey Girls looked like."

The photograph showed six young women standing on the porch.

"Fred Harvey was very strict about the girls' appearance and demanded that their uniforms always be clean, ironed, and identical. They wore long black skirts with long white aprons and black long-sleeve blouses with a white vest and collar. The senior girl would have the girls who were working that day stand in a line so she could measure their skirts, making sure they were exactly the same number of inches off the floor, and ensuring that their hair was perfectly combed and their caps level. Each girl was also required to wear a girdle, and the senior girl would actually thump their butts to make sure they had them on."

"I don't think I've ever seen a girdle," Jennifer said.

The three passed into the formal dining room through an opening whose double doors had been removed for refinishing. Large enough to hold two dozen round tables and chairs, its walls had been repaired, though the crew was still working on the twelve-foot ceiling.

"Our team worked in here during our first week,"

Jennifer told Mogi. "We peeled away layers of wallpaper, looking for the original stuff. We got pieces of the floor, removed some trim work, and then attacked the ceiling. The demolition crew took down the modern ceiling panels and found the original 1898-pressed tin tiles still in place. That was a real find. The owner plans to clean them up and leave them as the new ceiling.

"Anyway, the guests ate meals in this room as well as public visitors to the restaurant. Fred Harvey required men to wear suit coats with ties and ladies to have full skirts. We'd think it would be insane to ask customers to dress a certain way, but people back then enjoyed having dress-up restaurants that were like the fancy places back East. Fred did allow each restaurant to keep spare coats and ties for men who came unprepared."

Sue, picking up the story, explained, "Fred used the railroad to bring food from all over the US, including truffles, chocolates, maple syrup, mushrooms, fresh fish and clams, live turtles for fresh turtle soup, and fancy cuts of meat. He even offered genuine Cuban cigars for an after-dinner smoke. At a time when most eateries in the West brewed coffee once a day and then reheated it, Fred Harvey made a show out of his coffee urns being emptied every two hours and the coffee remade with fresh beans shipped from South America by way of Boston. The whole business—the food, the service, the facilities—made him famous across America. He became one of the wealthiest men in America by the turn of the century."

"Wow," Mogi said. "I wouldn't think that little ol' Las Vegas, New Mexico, would have been able to support something like that."

"You don't know Las Vegas," Sue said with a laugh.

"It was a rip-snorter of a town in the mid-1800s, right smack on the Santa Fe Trail, with outlaws and gunfighters and army forts and a whole host of famous people hanging around. Doc Holliday of Tombstone fame was a dentist here, and the building that held his office is still down by the town plaza. Of course, Wyatt Earp and his brothers passed through, as well as Kit Carson, Billy the Kid, and Pat Garrett. When the railroad came in 1879, Las Vegas started growing by leaps and bounds and eventually was bigger than either Santa Fe or Albuquerque. Wealthy railroad executives moved in, and the town developed a more civilized side.

"So when people went out to eat, the Harvey House at the Castañeda was the place to go, and they paid whatever was asked."

"Well, okay, but I still want to know about the ghosts," Mogi said. "Has anybody seen any for real? Is there a way we could walk around and see if any show up? Do you know any stories of the old times? If the hotel is remodeled so that it doesn't look so spooky, do you think the ghosts will leave?"

Sue laughed again. "You're still working on the ghosts, huh? Local history talks about gunfights in the street out front and people being shot in the hallways, so the hotel has the prerequisites for being haunted, but most stories I know about have strange sounds and lights and not ghosts. Of course, most of my sister's stories came from people who were probably drunk."

"We ought to come back at night," Mogi said. "Would they let us come back at night?"

"Don't even think about it," Jennifer told her brother with a frown. "We don't need any spooks or goblins. We have more than enough mysteries tracking down old women."

CHAPTER 5

"What? Who died?" Jennifer had gotten a confusing text from Mogi and was now walking through the door of his dorm room to find her brother leaning against scrunched-up pillows on his bed, his laptop propped up by his knees.

"Margaret Simpson, the owner of the footlocker," Mogi said as he looked up from his computer screen.

"She committed suicide in 1945. Right out on the railroad tracks. She waited until after dark and then stepped in front of a freight train."

"You're kidding! How did you find that out?"

"Remember the contact number you gave me for the Harvey Company? For tracking down the Harvey Girls? I've been exchanging emails with their No. 1 historian for all things Fred at the Belen Harvey House Museum, south of Albuquerque.

"This lady knew immediately who I was talking

about when I told her that a footlocker had been found with Margaret's stuff in it. She is very interested to hear what's inside, she may make a trip up here sometime. Margaret Simpson is apparently a legendary skeleton in Fred Harvey's closet."

"Do they know why she killed herself?"

"Not even a hint, but the information was fascinating. Margaret Simpson had worked as a Harvey Girl at the Harvey House in Williams, Arizona. She must have been really young, and she was single, of course —Harvey refused to hire married women or women with children.

"She worked as a regular Harvey Girl beginning in 1924. In 1931, she married one of the cooks, a guy named Matthew Turner. Since they were both employed by the company at the time, and it was during the Depression, the company bent the rules and allowed them both to continue working at the hotel as long as they lived in their own house.

"In 1935, Margaret Simpson shows up at the Castañeda in Las Vegas, applying for a position as senior girl. She says that her husband died, she had gone back to using her maiden name, and that they had no children. Since Margaret had years of experience and, at twenty-seven, was older than any of the Harvey Girls working at the hotel, she was hired.

"Ten years later, in 1945, on May 7, the official Fred Harvey records show that she supervised the shifts during the day and, that night, stepped onto the tracks just as a freight train was passing through. She didn't wear her big white apron, only her black blouse and black skirt, and the train's engineer said he never saw her until just before smacking into her.

"An investigation found that she was standing tall, facing the train, and put her hands over her eyes at the very last minute. It took almost a mile to get the train stopped and hours to find her body. It was reported that something terrible had happened that made her suddenly go crazy.

"Her death—her suicide—was hushed up because the company didn't want the publicity. The lady in Belen guessed that someone must have locked up her footlocker and put it in the attic.

"Now, here's the interesting part," Mogi said with raised eyebrows. "The lady in Belen says that Margaret Simpson didn't suddenly go crazy but had, in fact, carefully planned her death. She left a note on her bed with instructions for her burial, writing that she had bought a plot at the local cemetery and paid for an engraved headstone. But—and this is the zinger—not only did she pay for an engraved headstone but she had told the engraver the date of her death so the headstone would be completely finished before she died. That means she chose the date of her death a couple of weeks before it happened.

"She's buried in the Las Vegas cemetery. We ought to see if we can find her grave." Mogi went back to focusing on his screen.

"That's terrible!" Jennifer said. "It's bad enough thinking that she killed herself, but having chosen the date weeks beforehand? Now, that's spooky!"

"And by the way," Mogi said, "the historian lady said that the Fred Harvey Company keeps up on the names and addresses of all the women who had been employed as Harvey Girls and knows when somebody moves or dies. She told me how to get to the file, so we're home free for creating a mailing list."

CHAPTER 6

"It's my fault. I should have looked closer."

"It's not your fault," Mogi said to his sister from a prone position on the old bed. "I went over every item in the footlocker until my eyes fell out, and I missed it. I think it was my telling everybody that Margaret Simpson had planned her suicide that got the jerk all excited. Of course, I do wish I'd made the connection first. I'm supposed to be the big solver of mysteries, and I didn't even realize there was one."

The week before, while Mogi was working on the database for the reunion, Gabriel Sanchez from The Town Reporter asked to look at the footlocker. Although the Reporter, a small, student-produced publication with no university oversight, was not a respected media outlet, it seemed an innocent request, and the architecture department head thought it might garner more media attention for the school's summer intern programs.

Dr. Sanford had told Sue and Jennifer that she didn't read *that rag*, as she called it, because it sensationalized events. The girls were less apprehensive and expected no surprises because the locker and its contents had been examined, photographed, and handled by nearly all the assessment team's members, not to mention a reporter from the larger Las Vegas newspaper. Anything unusual would have already been found.

"We would be glad to show you the items," Dr. Sanford offered as she, Sue, Jennifer, and Sanchez entered the team room. He thanked her for the offer but said he'd prefer to look things over on his own.

The locker had been set on top of the bed, making it easier to access. After glancing quickly at the outside, Sanchez opened the lid and immediately took out the handful of newspapers.

The issues were from the daily edition of the Las Vegas Examiner. Las Vegas was not a large town after the Depression, and with the paper rationing of the war's early years, only one large rectangle of newsprint was used to print a four-page newspaper.

Sanchez laid out the papers according to date: October 17, 18, 19, 21, 24, and 30, and November 9.

After laying the papers open on the mattress, he examined each one, using his finger to carefully read each column heading and scan the text below it. If a particular column was interesting, he read every word. After laboriously going through the first newspaper, he spread it face down on the mattress and began the next.

Jennifer was a little suspicious as she watched and became concerned when Sanchez began to smile. She hadn't read much of the newspapers, figuring they just showed how boring it was to live in a small town in 1943. After quickly scanning them, she didn't find anything that shed light on Margaret Simpson or her job or even why she had kept the papers.

But Gabriel Sanchez was now smiling, nodding his head as he read, causing Jennifer to look at which articles seemed to be occupying his attention. They all concerned a robbery at a local bank.

Almost thirty minutes later, Sanchez finished the last paper and laid it on top of the others. "Why do you suppose she kept these newspapers?" he asked the three women, who had grown frustrated during his slow review.

Dr. Sanford did not respond. She was clearly irritated.

Jennifer knew she'd expected an interview, or at least a conversation, while he examined the footlocker's contents. None of them had anticipated waiting so long in silence or to be toyed with like this. If nothing else, Sanchez was rude.

"Why newspapers, and why these newspapers?" Sanchez continued. "It can't be incidental. There must be something that each of these papers contains that forms a progression of information, some reporting of an item that makes a continuing story."

He looked at the women's impassive faces. Getting no response, he went on.

"I found only one thing that is reported across all

of them. Well, actually two. There is always some kind of story about the war. Since the papers are from 1943, it would be remarkable if they didn't feature some news of the war.

"But," he smiled as he continued, "there is another story that continues in each issue. Look at the newspaper dated October 17."

He lifted the first paper from the stack and pointed to the front page. A headline read, "Las Vegas Bank Robbed."

He set the paper aside and then held up the October 18 issue, again displaying the front page and pointing to a similar headline: "No Robbers Found Yet. Police Intensify Hunt."

He laid the paper aside and then went through the rest.

The October 19 issue had a similar story, but its headline was smaller and off to the right, the main headline now concerned war news from the Pacific. Over the next four issues, with no new developments, the bank robbery stories grew less and less prominent. Sanchez finished with the November 9 issue and laid the stack back on the mattress. "Let me summarize the incident that all of these articles refer to," he said.

"The Las Vegas State Bank was robbed by two men a few minutes before noon on October 16, 1943. The two robbers were dressed identically in new denim coveralls, new cotton work shirts buttoned to their necks, and what appeared to be new broad-brimmed hats. Both had pistols that appeared to be of the same make, model, and caliber. Both wore shined shoes. Both carried silver pocket watches on silver chains. The men were nervous but methodical.

"Surprisingly, the two men were twins. Not one man in the bank noticed, but several of the women recognized it immediately. The eyes, the nose, the mouth, the mannerisms—there was no doubt in their minds.

"According to the senior clerk of the bank, a Mr. Harold Lennon, the men obviously knew what they were doing. Each constantly checked his pocket watch as if on a definite schedule. They knew that a large quantity of newly issued hundred-dollar bills had been delivered from a Kansas City bank that morning, and they even knew that the bills would be out in the open, being sorted on a table in the vault.

"Once the bank employees and customers were subdued, Lennon was forced into the vault and instructed to put those new hundred-dollar bills into a large, green sack that the bandits had brought with them. Then they were all moved into the vault, and the door closed.

"And the two men vanished into thin air. No one on the streets near the bank saw any strangers running from the scene. No unknown car or other vehicle was seen leaving the area. Roadblocks led to many vehicles being searched, but nothing unusual was found. All close-by trash cans and dumpsters were searched, but no clothes, no bags, no pistols, no hats—nothing was found.

"Over the next week, there was no increased

spending at local businesses or nearby towns, and no one came forward with information. There wasn't a whiff of the robbers.

"The case baffled everyone. As with all good crimes, nothing ever turned up. Years went by. The story eventually grew into another obscure legend of New Mexico, which, of course, means it was turned into a draw for tourists.

"I imagine the November article was the last one about the robbery. The money was replaced by the federal bank, and there was a war on. The citizens of Las Vegas had enough to occupy their minds."

The last part was obviously his summary of the situation, but Sanchez wasn't done with his sleuthing. "Why did she keep these newspapers? The only common element is the story of the robbery. Why did she not keep more papers? She didn't kill herself until 1945—that's two years, a lot of newspapers not to keep. So why did she keep only these papers? Because our Margaret Simpson was interested in how the story was developing.

"I think she knew that if the robbery was not solved within a few weeks, it would never be solved. If the newspaper stopped reporting about it, then Margaret Simpson knew she was safe."

Jennifer couldn't help herself. "Uh—what? Wait a minute. You think having these newspapers, or the lack of having more newspapers, means that Margaret Simpson knew something about the robbery? That she was involved?"

Sanchez looked at her and tilted his head. "Well,"

he began, but then stopped. Reaching inside the foot-locker, he grabbed two items and held them up. The silver pocket watches.

Just like the watches the two men had been seen repeatedly checking as the robbery progressed.

"Really?" Sue said. "You think those two pocket watches were the ones used by the robbers?" She turned to Dr. Sanford.

"We can't know that," the professor said coldly.

None of them knew the story of the bank robbery, including Dr. Sanford. She had lived in Las Vegas for several years and knew many of the local legends and myths, especially if they were connected to a particular house or the library or a building on the Plaza, but if she had heard the legend of the bank robbery, she had forgotten it.

Nonetheless, she objected to Sanchez's smug tone and his hasty conclusions.

Jennifer was disgusted. The idea that Margaret Simpson was being connected to a crime without any real evidence was wrong. She was a Harvey Girl. No Harvey Girl could have done such a thing, and certainly no senior girl. She felt as if Margaret Simpson—and Fred Harvey himself—were being slapped in the face.

Sanchez returned to the locker, rummaging through the other items. He picked up the Bible, looked it over, examined the carved leather cover, and held the lacing close to his face. He opened the Bible, flipped through the pages, and then studied the binding.

"We're done here," Dr. Sanford said, rising from her chair.

Ignoring her, Sanchez arched the binding back and pulled the front and back covers out of their leather sleeves.

Several one-hundred-dollar bills fluttered to the floor.

CHAPTER 7

The Town Reporter

Mystery of Famous Bank Robbery Solved!

Monday, July 10—The greatest Las Vegas mystery in history has finally been solved.

An ancient footlocker belonging to Margaret Simpson, a longtime Fred Harvey Company employee who worked as the senior girl at the Castañeda Hotel, was found in a hidden attic room a few weeks ago.

The footlocker was first celebrated as a fortuitous historical find but quickly became the key to understanding and solving an enduring Las Vegas legend. Opening the locker revealed several issues of the Las Vegas Examiner, dated from October 17, 1943, the day after the famous robbery at the Las Vegas State Bank, through November 9.

The story of the robbery was a clear common element among the newspapers. That such an obvious connection existed among the articles threw a light on the reasons for their being kept together in the footlocker, and a more intensive inspection of the other items was begun.

Two silver pocket watches were found in the locker and immediately became suspect. Witnesses unfortunate enough to be in the bank that morning gave a detailed description of each of the robbers looking at a silver pocket watch as if the men were on a firm timetable. The watches in the footlocker match exactly the descriptions of the pocket watches used by the bandits on the day of the robbery.

Those watches alone provide damning evidence that there existed a confederacy between the owner of the footlocker and the robbers who pulled off that heinous crime so long ago.

But that's not all. Further examination of the footlocker's contents brought to light Margaret Simpson's Bible. A search of the Bible revealed that several crisp one-hundred-dollar bills had been secreted inside the leather cover.

After almost eighty years without so much as a single hint of what happened that day, it is now obvious that an innocent-looking, well-respected, and hard-working Harvey Girl was, in fact, the black-hearted leader of a gang that pulled off what would become the biggest unsolved crime in New Mexico history. It was an act by dastardly criminals, devoid of mercy and compassion.

It would have taken ruthless, daring, and calculating villains to steal money from the poverty-stricken hands of the Las Vegas community. That a Harvey Girl was the center of such a venture is hardly imaginable.

Questions still remain: Who were the two robbers hired by

this devilish woman? Did she hide the thieves in the Castañeda itself until the pressure was off? What happened to the money? Did she squander it while still pretending to be a lowly waitress?

How many other people were involved in this crime? How big a gang did she have? Was it morbid curiosity that led her to keep the newspaper articles, or was it pride in her accomplishment?

It is well-known to the Fred Harvey Company that Margaret Simpson later committed suicide by throwing herself under the wheels of a freight train.

Was it an overwhelming sense of guilt that drove her to commit suicide in 1945? Or did she just run out of money and couldn't face being poor again?

This reporter will keep you informed as the investigation continues.

"It's been days since I've read this, and I still feel like I'm going to vomit," Mogi said, tossing the thin newspaper back to Jennifer. "He's making it all up. Mystery solved? Really? Black-hearted woman? Leader of the gang? I didn't know anyone used the word *dastardly* anymore. What kind of newspaper would print this trash?"

"I used to read the Reporter all the time, but I quit," Sue said. "They just make stuff up and then make it sound earth-shattering. I asked one of my English professors about it, and he told me Gabriel Sanchez is actually a student working on his master's degree in English.

"The Town Reporter doesn't exist outside of the guy's computer in the basement of his mother's house. He writes articles using different names so you think it's a big operation, adds in some local news that he takes from the real Las Vegas newspaper, and then sends the files to some website that formats all the articles in a heading and column format. He shoots the result to a cheap print shop here in town, and they produce a one-page, hand-it-out-on-street-corners type of newspaper. It's not even published on a regular basis, he only puts out a paper when he's got new lies that he thinks people will get excited about. In short, he's a low-life masquerading as a journalist."

"Why do people read it?" Jennifer asked in surprise.

Sue shrugged. "People know it's a garbage paper, but it's entertaining. Besides, this is New Mexico, where people are stand-up proud of space alien visits."

"What gets me," Jennifer added, shaking her head, "is that he seemed to know he was going to find something."

He spent half an hour connecting the articles about the robbery, reached directly in the footlocker for the pocket watches, and then tore the cover off the Bible, all while ignoring the other stuff.

She looked at Mogi. "You, at least, noticed that the letters were missing."

The Reporter article had come out on Monday, and it was now Friday afternoon. After coming back from lunch, the three young people were in the team room upstairs in the Castañeda. Sue sat at a table working at a computer, Jennifer was puttering among the boxes, and Mogi lay stretched out on the mattress, fighting to keep his eyes open.

Over the past month, the room's floor had grown increasingly cluttered with boxes full of artifacts, a hand-painted chest from one of the hotel rooms, an open box of plumbing fixtures, mirrors leaning against a wall, light fixtures hanging from the wood-work above the closet, curtains draped over hangers suspended from the window frame, plus other mate-rials that made up the team's mini-museum.

The clutter allowed only a small path through the piles of assorted relics, winding from the computer table on one end of the room to the bed at the other end.

Mogi had used the Fred Harvey Company's

employee database to build a spreadsheet from which he had generated a contact list, printed out address labels, and sent the invitations, all by the end of his first week with the team. Many of the *girls* had already passed away or were unable to travel, but nearly twenty had enthusiastically accepted the invitation.

The Castañeda open house was two weeks away, on the last Saturday of July. Dr. Sanford's class needed to finish the assessment, complete the team's information binder, finalize the report, and build the lobby display for the reunion. Their semester final would be given the first week of August.

It would then be back to the hot slickrock country of Utah for Mogi and Jennifer.

"Hello? Anybody home?"

They all jumped at the sound of a deep male voice and saw a distinguished, older black man at the door.

"Hello, I'm looking for Sue or Jennifer," he said.

"You've come to the right place," Sue said as she ushered him in. "I'm Sue, this is Jennifer, and this is Mogi, Jennifer's brother."

"Colonel John Hurley," the man introduced himself as he shook their hands. "I believe these belong to you."

He handed Sue the bundle of letters from the footlocker. "I expect you're about to become nationally famous, so the history department decided we'd best get everything back together. Dr. Sanford told me you might be over here, so I thought I'd drop them off."

"Nationally famous?" Jennifer asked. "What does that mean?"

The man smiled. "The letters. It's an unusual event to find a group of previously undiscovered letters written during World War II. Most war correspondence was found years ago and has been researched until people are tired of talking about it, so historians get pretty excited to find something new. I finished putting up the images on the department's website at the end of June, and we're already seeing all sorts of emails and Facebook posts with comments and analyses. At least one history journal has already shown an interest in publishing a paper on them. Once the word goes further, there will probably be a deluge of responses. You might be giving a lot of interviews."

The three young people were stunned.

"Uh, like, what did the letters have in them that makes them so interesting?" Mogi asked.

"Well, in my opinion," the man said smiling, "they were pretty ordinary except for a few quirks."

"Like what?" Jennifer asked.

"Well, there aren't any envelopes, for one thing. Not having any postal marks, combined with the fact that the writer never wrote the date inside the letters, means we can't be sure when the letters were written or in what order they were written. Even more odd, though, is that the top of each letter was cut off. If it weren't for the salutation at the beginning of each letter, we wouldn't even know to whom they were sent."

"Excuse me," Mogi said with a questioning look,

"but addresses aren't usually included inside a letter anyway if it's a personal letter."

Colonel Hurley took one of the letters from the bundle he had given Sue, unfolded it, and held it up.

"Yes, but these aren't ordinary letters. In any overseas conflict, mailing letters back and forth between family members and soldiers is a big problem. How do you know where a soldier is going to be? What kind of postal system exists where the soldier is? What kind of stamps would be needed? Postal systems wouldn't be operating in combat zones, anyway.

"During World War II, there were approximately three million allied soldiers all over Europe. If everyone was writing letters, that's a complicated business for different countries with different languages, different mail systems, and sometimes no governments. So the army invented its own system."

He pointed at the letter. "This is called a V-mail letter, which is short for Victory Mail. The soldier would write the name and address of whoever he was sending it to, write his own military address next to it, and then write his message between the margins in the space below. Only the front side of the page was used, which meant that writers were limited to a pretty small space. When finished, the letter was folded a certain way and put into an envelope that had a cut-out opening to show the recipient's address.

"The letters were gathered up by the army units and sent to central locations where the army postal service would take each one out, lay it flat, photograph it using a high-speed movie camera—at one frame per letter—and then send the film back to the States. A single sack of movie film could hold a hundred fifty thousand letters, compared to the thirty-seven sacks that would have been needed for that many regular letters.

"When the movie film reached America, each frame of the film was projected onto a page of light-sensitive paper, which recreated the letter as it had originally been written. The letter was then refolded and put into another envelope, again with the address showing, and mailed through the regular US mail system. It was a happy day when a wife got a letter from her husband or a mom got a letter from her son.

"If Mom wanted to write back, she did the same thing but in reverse: She got a V-mail form from the post office, wrote the letter, and sent it by way of regular US mail. The letter was free for military personnel, though it cost Mom three cents. The US Postal Service intercepted the V-mail letters and gave them to the army, which then did the same filming process. The letter would eventually be delivered to the army unit where the soldier was stationed.

"It worked really well. In World War II, between 1942 and 1946, more than 556 million V-mail letters were sent by soldiers, generating 510 million V-mail letters back.

"So," he said, pointing to the space above the letter in his hand, "this is where Mom's address would have appeared, and right next to it would have been the address of the soldier writing the letter. In this case, whoever received it cut off the top of the letter."

"Why would Margaret have done that?" Mogi asked.

Colonel Hurley smiled. "That's a good question. We don't have a clue. Now, another thing that seems strange is that, other than her name, there are never any real names used. The handwriting is all the same, so it was the same person, and that person had a cousin, but the writer of the letter uses the nickname of *Wyatt* and his cousin is referred to as *Doc*. We assume those were not their real names."

"You're kidding!" Sue exclaimed. "Wyatt Earp and Doc Holliday?"

Colonel Hurley laughed. "It's got to be. Don't ask me why."

Mogi stood up, suddenly excited. "This sounds really weird. What did the letters say? I mean, was somebody just sending goofy letters?"

"Ah, another good question. In fact, the letters tell what the two soldiers were experiencing in an honest, forthright way. *Wyatt* holds nothing back and is obviously used to talking to Mrs. Simpson in a personal way. The army typically cautioned soldiers not to be too truthful when they wrote home. If a soldier wrote about something terrible happening, like being shot at or having bombs go off, even if it was a daily occurrence, it could be frightening and upsetting to somebody reading it in the middle of, say, Ohio. It's a bad deal to scare your mother, so you want to keep everything nice if you can.

"Not so with Wyatt. He writes about what he sees and, more importantly, how he feels. You should read these letters if you haven't already. But better to look at the images on the department website rather than handling the originals since the letters are almost eighty years old and are pretty fragile. I've already had to fight off people who wanted to mount them under plexiglass in the library."

CHAPTER 8

t was Sunday afternoon when Jennifer walked into her brother's dorm room. She found him standing and staring at five sheets of paper he had taped to the wall.

"What are you doing?"

Mogi frowned. "I printed the letters off the website, and I'm trying to understand what I'm looking at. I'm examining them a few at a time so I can focus on each one, hoping I'll see something I haven't seen yet."

Jennifer had read them and she too couldn't quite get past what Colonel Hurley had called *quirks*. She looked at the letters Mogi had taped up, each now marked up with underlining, exclamation points, circles around individual words, and penciled-in notes.

Ignoring his artwork, she read through them again.

Dear Mrs. Margaret Simpson,

The first that we saw of Europe was when we were watching Higgins boats land on the beach. They are not much more than a deep, rectangular box of wood with a propeller and a ramp that flops down in the front. It's big, though, enough to hold thirty or so, plus the Coast Guard guys driving it. I guess you learn to run, swim, or wade as fast as you can when that ramp goes down because some German is going to be shooting at you. Doc and I were in a bigger flat-bottomed landing ship waiting for the tide to go down so we could walk down a gangway onto the beach.

We didn't go in until the second day of the invasion, so we didn't get shot at like the first guys on the beach, which was a good thing because I saw a lot of their dead bodies floating in the waves. More than 6,000 ships were used on the first day, and there were still that many offshore when we were there, all the freighters and landing ships waiting to settle onto the sand and unload. The tide comes and goes twice a day, so the landing ships have to pull up in the water and wait for the tide to go out so they can open the big doors on the front end and let out the trucks, artillery, tanks, cranes, bulldozers, and such, and get it all done before the tide comes back and they start to float again.

Doc and I were in a half-track, so we didn't even get wet.

Don't worry that we're finally in the war. We will be okay.

Wyatt and Doc.

Dear Mrs. Margaret Simpson,

Doc, my older cousin, and I want to make sure that you did what we told you to do with regard to the holy scripture. We want you to be taken care of. We don't know exactly where we are right now, or even the date, but that's okay because I think the war is pretty much the same no matter where we are. We want to stay in our half-track, but sometimes it can't make it across the fields or through the bushes, so we have to get out and fight on foot. Duck and cover, duck and cover. You'd think that our officers would trust us to take care of ourselves and to protect the people in our squad. Doc is more gung-ho than me, which is a word that our sergeants have been telling us we ought to have more of, so they are pretty impressed with him. I think if you have a lot of gung-ho then you are out in front of any charge we make, and that seems like a poor place to be to me. I'll follow Doc and let him go gung-ho first.

Wyatt and Doc.

Dear Mrs. Margaret Simpson,

We're in the middle of it now. I don't know if you heard what the army did, but let's just say that we hit the Germans in a really big way—bombers and fighters and such—and we've got them backing up. Lots of fighting, but we are winning most everything. I thought I was ready to keep after them, but everything gets confusing because of all the bullets flying. It rains a lot here and there's a whole lot more mud than back home, and our trucks get stuck a lot. The half-track is better, but it can get stuck sometimes too. The air stinks because of all the smoke from the tanks and trucks and the big pieces of artillery, besides the fact that we're fighting in fields where cows have left a lot of manure. It's also noisy from the artillery being shot all the time and the tanks going by and the mortars going off. It's hard going, so we stay close to the tanks, which is a good thing. The ground shakes too. And there's always bombers going over. I don't like this much and even Doc, my older cousin, is getting the heebie-jeebies. I never knew that people could be so violent toward each other.

Wyatt and Doc.

Dear Mrs. Margaret Simpson,

We first came into France in the lowlands. A lot of fields and pastures and hedges in between were hard to fight through. But we got past them and we're into rolling hills now, so the going is easier and we spend more time in our trucks. That walking every-where and getting nowhere was troubling me. Doc, my older cousin, and I are part of a half-track crew. That's a big vehicle that's like a truck but it has tracks like a tank in the back and two wheels like a truck up front and they have a big machine gun mounted behind the driver so they can get up a head of steam and break through barriers while still killing the enemy.

Doc and I get in the back and we're supposed to use our rifles to shoot the enemy from behind and get them when they're shooting down on us from the rooftops where the big machine gun can't turn to shoot high enough. We have worked out a system that keeps us from getting killed. We let the other people stand up to shoot over the sides of the half-track and then wait for thirty seconds to let them get killed if anybody is going to get killed, and then we pop up behind them and shoot the high places where the Krauts are. Don't worry about us. We are watching out for each other.

Wyatt and Doc.

Dear Mrs. Margaret Simpson,

There's lots of dead people here. There are special soldiers who follow the front lines and gather up the bodies and take them to places where they can be buried. They try to do it fast so that the soldiers who come afterward don't see the bodies and get discouraged or frightened. They put the bodies in mattress covers and tie them up and put them in shallow graves to be dug up later when they buy land to make a permanent cemetery that can be used for military soldiers. They put a white wooden cross in the ground where the grave is. I've already seen hundreds of white *crosses in a hundred different places. Nobody will tell us how many men are dying and maybe they don't know, but it's a lot. I wonder how many cemeteries are behind us.*

I got wounded, but it's nothing. My foxhole was too close to a mortar round and it exploded and a piece of shrapnel caught me right under the helmet, cutting the back of my head and making a lot of blood spurt out. It took some stitches, but I'm okay. I went back to my company after a day at the aid station, which was nice because I could lie down stretched out, which you can't do in a foxhole. Nothing to worry about.

Don't worry about us. Doc and I have been together a long, long time, being cousins and all, and we know how to stick with each other.

Wyatt and Doc.

"I don't get the *Dear Mrs. Margaret Simpson* business," Jennifer said as she finished the letters.

"Me neither. It's hard enough to read because of the rambling sentences. I guess he's always in a hurry because he spends his life in a foxhole or a half-track. Who are these guys, anyway? We don't know the dates, but I'm guessing the letters span a year or two.

You'd think that Wyatt would use *Mrs. Simpson* or her first name, but not both. And why did they use fake names anyway? Who would care what their real names were?"

"And how come Doc never wrote anything?" Jennifer asked. "Of course, we don't know that he didn't. We don't even know if we have all the letters that she got. There could have been a bunch of letters that were lost or destroyed. And we don't even know their sequence. I would guess that Wyatt talking about the ship would have been when he and Doc landed in Normandy, but we don't really know. I wish we had the dates."

"They seem all screwed up to me," Mogi said. "I can't figure out if Wyatt is dumb or just doesn't write well. Or maybe it's being surrounded by the war that makes him jumble everything together. Did she meet these guys in the restaurant one day as they were passing through and they started writing to her? Maybe they didn't have anybody else? Could they have been the kids of some friend of hers? But one of them was a cousin to the other—an older cousin, he repeatedly says—so they weren't brothers. I don't understand any of it. It might help if we knew how old they were, but I guess all the soldiers were young, maybe even teenagers."

Mogi huffed. "I'm just not connecting here."

Sue walked into the room. "Hey, look at what some Harvey Girl sent Dr. Sanford. She brought it over to me."

CHAPTER 9

t was a large photograph, obviously old, in a thick, black paper frame that had been embossed to make it look like leather, with gold embroidery around the edges. There was a photographer's stamp in the corner.

Thirty or so people stood lined up next to a large cottonwood tree. There were two rows of Harvey Girls, all dressed in black skirts that almost touched the ground and long-sleeved black blouses, each with a long white apron that covered the front of her blouse and nearly all of her skirt, extending to just a few inches above the bottom hem.

Several men stood on top of a wall behind the women, wearing cooks' uniforms—white pants, white long-sleeved shirts, white aprons, and white caps with no brims. On the left side of the photo, two men in suits stood a foot or so away, and there were also a couple of younger men in different uniforms kneeling. A stern-looking man in a three-piece suit and a bowler hat stood behind them. Next to him was a Harvey Girl standing separately from the others.

Numbers had been inked in above several of the people.

"The lady who sent this said it was taken in 1943. I've got the list that corresponds to the numbers. That Harvey Girl standing to the left is Margaret Simpson. The guy in the bowler hat is Jack Morris, the manager of the hotel. The men in the white uniforms worked in the kitchen and bakery, the two men in suits worked behind the counter in the lobby, and the younger men were porters."

Mogi scanned the people as Sue identified them, but he kept coming back to the image of Margaret Simpson. She was petite, shorter than he had imagined, and pretty. Her dark hair was rolled and tied into a bun behind her head, and she wore a folded, white, shell-shaped band tucked into her hair above her forehead like the other women. She did not wear an apron.

"She doesn't look like a dastardly bank robber to me," Mogi said quietly, "no matter what Gabriel Sanchez says."

When Sanchez had left, after doing his damage to the Bible, Dr. Sanford carefully put the leather cover back on the book, placed it in the footlocker, and snapped the lid shut. She gathered up the bills, saying she would bring them to the dean. Then she gave Sue and Jennifer a ride back to the dorm and drove off in a huff.

Sue and Jennifer hadn't known what to think.

Being bested by a jerk like Sanchez was one thing, but finding the bills had upset their impression of Margaret Simpson.

She was a Harvey Girl—a senior Harvey Girl—who had worked hard at her job and must have been good at it. Everything about her should have been top-notch and respectable. But taken at face value, the watches, the newspaper articles, and the bills built quite a case: Margaret Simpson was connected in some way to the bank robbery of 1943.

After they got back and shared the details with Mogi, the three friends were left not knowing quite how to paint a picture of what had happened, a picture that had suddenly gone askew.

"She doesn't look like a robber because she wasn't one," Jennifer said with a defiant tone, peering at Margaret's face in the photograph. "She can't have done it. She would have been swamped at the restaurant. She certainly wouldn't have had time to make herself look like a man, go over to the bank, pull off the robbery, and then hide everything afterward."

"Oh, I agree with that," Mogi said. "I don't think there's any way she was one of the robbers. How could she have looked like a twin to the other guy? But that doesn't mean she wasn't involved. She could have planned it or helped the two men to escape or something."

"What if," Sue said, "she didn't have anything to do with the robbery but saw something afterward? Maybe she saw the two guys run out of the bank and get into a car. Maybe the two guys knew she had seen them, so they gave her money to stay quiet. That would explain the bills. It was hard times—a few hundred could have made a major difference in anybody's life."

"What about the watches?" Mogi asked. "I doubt the guys would have given her their watches. Even if something happened between them, we're talking a small number of minutes that they had to escape in. That's not enough time to convince a bystander to not say anything."

"You're assuming that the two watches in the foot-locker are the ones used by the robbers," Sue said. "We don't know that."

Mogi tipped his head side to side a couple of times.

"That's true, but that kind of coincidence seems unlikely. I don't believe in coincidences myself."

"Well, I think we should go with Margaret Simpson not having anything to do with the robbery," Jennifer said. "I just can't imagine that she did. It must have been like Sue said, that she saw something. Maybe the crooks came back sometime later and gave her the money. Maybe, in fact, they came back in 1945 and threatened her, and that's why she killed herself."

"On the other hand," Sue said, "maybe she hid the money for the bank robbers, and they came back in 1945 to get it. Think of all the places inside the Castañeda where you could hide a sack of money. She could have siphoned off a little for expenses and hidden some bills in her Bible."

The three friends spent the rest of the day wandering between their dorm rooms to stew about the mess that Sanchez had stirred up. Now, with the letters bringing up new questions about why some soldier was writing to Margaret Simpson, the three were stymied, each sorting through a load of random facts and guesses about who and what the senior girl really was.

"Is it time to quit yet?" Mogi finally asked. "It is Sunday night, you know. We should be giving our brains time to relax, and I'm starving. Is anybody else starving? Can we go eat?"

"It's almost six," Sue said. "How about enchiladas at Mike's Café?"

"Oh, I definitely could do that," Jennifer said.

"Hey, I've got an even better idea," Mogi added.

"How about enchiladas and then we go to the hotel?"

"What happened to resting our brains? There's no way I'm doing any more work," Sue said. "I'm toast."

"Work? Who said work?" Mogi replied. "I don't mean going back to do work. How about we go ghost hunting? I've been slaving for you two for weeks and have resisted all thoughts of checking out the ghosts at the hotel, and now half the summer is gone. You have a set of keys to the building, right? Let's sneak in and see if we can hear any spooky voices or mysterious footsteps going down the hallways. I'd give anything to see one of those bouncy balls of light."

CHAPTER 10

Jennifer had walked how many times through the hotel?

After six weeks of searching the nooks and crannies, examining every room from the attic to the basement, she figured she could walk through the hotel after dark without being scared. It should have been as familiar to her as the Franklin home back in Bluff.

She was wrong.

Under the cloak of darkness, with clouds over the moon, no electric lights, and only flashlight beams bouncing off the surfaces, the typically boring hallways had been transformed into long, narrow tunnels veiled in shadow, each side room a hiding place for serial killers, the empty doorways an invitation to lurking beasts, while the openings of fallen ceiling plaster held nooses ready to snag those who passed beneath. The hundred-year-old wood flooring that had routinely creaked and squeaked now moaned and sighed, carrying what sounded like warnings of danger ahead.

She swore that she heard footsteps behind them.

"Okay, I'm done," Jennifer said, the trio having finished creeping around the second story, shining their lights into each room, flashing them against the walls and ceilings, and then going back down into the lobby. The stairway seemed secure and wide enough not to hide any goblins, but the only light coming into the lobby was from outside street lamps, leaving dark corners that were obvious hiding places for deranged zombies.

Mogi turned and placed his flashlight under his chin so that only the highlights of his face were seen, changing his face into that of a ghoul. "But we've waited such a long time for you to come," he said in a deepened voice, letting out an eerie laugh at the end.

"Come on," Sue said with a squeal. "We can't quit now. We haven't made it to the kitchen, where ghostly knives are supposed to shoot across the room. I want to be able to tell my sister that I walked the whole place without freaking out."

The three continued their survey downstairs, wandering around the lunchroom, peeking into the horribly stained bathrooms, and hurrying through the narrow cloakroom. They had yet to find any ghostly apparitions, feel cold drafts against their faces, see mysterious globes of light, or glimpse faint faces peering through the windows.

They hurried past the stairway and crossed into the dining room.

"Let's pick a place and see if anything comes to us," Mogi said in a hushed voice, moving to a back corner.

The other two joined him and each sank to the floor with their backs against the wall, turning their flashlights off. They snuggled together for both warmth and courage, comforted that at least nothing could surprise them from behind.

Over the next few minutes, between making noises themselves when they stretched, Mogi burping several times, and all three laughing at their own fright, they sat still and listened to the darkness. In spite of their playful attitude, the silence slowly grew more intense.

A stiff breeze was blowing outside, making the bushes scrape against the west windows, creating a scratchy sound that echoed against the far wall. The light from the streetlights filtered through the leaves of the cottonwoods, leaving disconnected spots of light against the walls and floor, and when the trees swayed, the shadows made erratic patterns. The occasional car driving past on the street swept jumbled lights around the room.

A bat, or maybe a captive bird, made a beating noise above them someplace in the attic, or was it in a guest room upstairs?

Smells were stronger: sawdust, plaster, floor polish, glue on new molding, fresh paint on window sills. The three could even smell their own clothes. Mogi swore he smelled the quilt from the footlocker.

Faintly, after nearly an hour had passed, new sounds echoed in the room. A hard thump, like something had been dropped on a floor. A scraping sound —maybe a window or door being opened?—followed by silence.

As ready as they were to run screaming for the front door, the three friends sat as if glued to the old linoleum squares beneath them, their eyes straining to see any movement in the confusing light.

A hammer blow sounded. Mogi was certain he recognized the distinct ring of metal against metal. One blow, then another. A pause. Another blow. Rocks, maybe gravel scraping somewhere.

A cough.

That's when Mogi decided they needed to investigate.

"Are you kidding?" Jennifer said in a panicked whisper.

"Ghosts don't cough."

"You can't be serious."

"It's no ghost," Mogi said, keeping his voice down.

"Somebody is in the basement. I don't know how they got there, but we ought to at least go to the basement door and listen. Somebody's down there, and we know they shouldn't be."

Sue squirmed, clearly spooked. "You're wrong! Nobody could be down there because nobody can get down there. We've only done one walkthrough to look for furniture, and then it was declared off-limits and locked. And remember me telling you that the outside basement entrance, the one with the slanted door, has a welded bar across it? It can't be opened!"

There was another hammer blow, then silence.

"Uh...wait a minute," Sue said. "I forgot about the utility tunnels."

Mogi looked at her, eyes wide. "Tunnels?"

"Remember you asked about that building on the other side of the yard from the north wing? The steam house, where they make steam to heat the hotel and the depot? They run steam pipes underground to each building through underground tunnels. If you can get into the tunnels at the steam house, you can get into the hotel basement."

"We're talking big tunnels?" Mogi asked.

"Well, I haven't been in them, but my sister said that students used to get into parties in the hotel by going through the tunnels, so they must be big enough to walk through."

"Let's go look for them!" Mogi whispered excitedly.

"Are you kidding?" Jennifer shouted in a whisper.

"You've got Frankenstein's monster in the basement with a hammer, and you want to go down there?"

"Uh...yeah, now's probably not a good time," Mogi admitted. "Maybe we can go tomorrow, when—"

"We can't go at all, remember?" Sue interrupted him.

"I've got a key, but the basement is off-limits to anybody but the construction crew. I only came tonight because you two have worked so hard that I thought a little adventure would be a fun reward."

Mogi took a deep breath, rolled his eyes, and tried a new tactic. "But the monster might have also broken through the back door. We ought to check it out if nothing else."

"I'll only go if we agree to call the police if we have even the tiniest suspicion of something wrong," Jennifer said.

"Absolutely," he replied.

"Deal," Sue agreed.

Moving slowly, straining to quiet their breathing, the trio crept into the kitchen. The hammer blows continued at irregular intervals but grew fainter, as if whoever was doing it had moved farther away. A moment later, the noises stopped.

The three paused at the silence and then crept across the kitchen floor into a hallway, turned right, and rounded a corner. As quiet as they tried to be, every step brought a squeak from the floor.

After another turn in the hallway, they stopped, bunched up tight, and looked straight ahead at the delivery door and the roll-up garage door next to it. On their left was the hallway door that led to the basement.

Mogi carefully stepped to the delivery door. He grabbed the handle and gave it a tug. It was locked.

While Sue shined her flashlight across it, he also confirmed that the garage door was locked.

Mogi turned his attention to the basement door.

"Since you can't open it from the other side," he whispered, "whoever is in there had to come through the tunnels you were talking about. But at this time of night, why?" He ran his light across the top, down each side, and across the bottom. Nothing unusual.

Motioning his companions closer, he placed his hand flat against the top panel of the door and pressed his ear up against the wood.

Sue and Jennifer scrunched up next to him, and soon, three ears were pressed closely against the door.

At first, they heard no sound. Then, faintly at first and soon growing stronger, there was a slight whooshing sound, a rhythmic in-and-out. In-and-out. In-and-out.

Only when they heard a stifled sneeze did their chests explode.

The three adventurers took off running. Around the corner, down the hallway, across the kitchen, through the dining room, and out the front door. Sue barely remembered to stop and lock it.

The whooshing sound had been someone breathing on the other side of the door, leaning up against it, listening to them as they listened to—it.

CHAPTER 11

D

r. Sanford was waiting for them in the dining hall early the next morning.

"Do you have the keys to the building?" she asked Sue before the three could sit down. They glanced at each other nervously. Had their sneaking into the hotel last night been discovered?

Struggling to look alert and studently, Sue rummaged through her daypack, found the keys in a side pocket, and handed them over. "What's up?"

"The construction trailer was broken into last night. They believe the only thing taken was a set of backup keys, like these. They're afraid somebody will vandalize the hotel or steal the equipment, so the construction manager is changing the locks on the outside doors. I'll get a new set to you soon. Until then, you'll have to hunt down one of the crew and borrow a key to get in the team room.

"Just in case, why don't you bring the binder to my office," Dr. Sanford said. "We ought to keep them locked up from now on. Maybe you should also gather up any unique artifacts and bring them up here too. Everybody doing okay? You all look tired."

Sue perked up and smiled. "Oh, we're fine."

"We should bring the footlocker," Jennifer said. "It's pretty unique. We could get it now and bring it to class and then put it in your office."

"That's a good idea—we couldn't replace its contents. See you in class."

After she walked away, the three friends slumped into their chairs. Mogi laid his head on the table. "I feel awful. I didn't sleep at all. I kept hearing somebody breathing in my ears."

After barely staying awake through breakfast, they drove to the Castañeda.

———

The footlocker was gone.

Sue had opened the padlock on the door with a borrowed key, and they now stood in the room, shocked.

There was an empty space on the mattress.

"That's why the keys were stolen!" Mogi said, fully revived by the scent of a crime. "Whoever took them wanted to steal the footlocker. They must have broken into the trailer after we left last night. But why take it? We'd almost worn the hinges off making the contents public. The letters are probably valuable, but they're posted on the internet, so how could they be worth breaking into the building?"

"Well," Jennifer said, "maybe for souvenirs? The footlocker has become pretty famous, thanks to us. And the letters might be valuable to a collector of war stuff."

Mogi huffed. She was right. There could be several people still alive who knew Margaret, knew what had happened to her, and might want something as a memory—her Bible perhaps. But someone in their 80s or 90s probably couldn't break into the construction trailer, and they certainly couldn't carry the footlocker down the stairs. They would have needed an accomplice.

Then there were the watches—they were certainly antiques. And the locker itself. There might be a code or something marked inside that he had missed, or a map made by overlapping the newspaper articles. Maybe even invisible ink on the papers, giving a clue about something. What if the message was heat-activated? How about something that should have been in the footlocker but wasn't, like socks, underwear, or a nightshirt? Could something that wasn't there be a key to explaining the rest of it?

An idea smacked him in the head.

"Oh, man!" he exclaimed.

"What?" Jennifer said.

"There might be something written on the bottom of the footlocker! I never thought to look there."

Sue and Jennifer looked at each other. They had taken pictures inside and out but had never thought about turning the locker over to look at the bottom.

But what could possibly be on the bottom that would make any difference?

They nodded in silent agreement that it didn't matter.

"Well, we've got to get back to class," Sue said, looking at her phone. "Dr. Sanford is going to have a fit when we tell her the footlocker has been taken. The papers, photos, and everything else I've done are backed up to the cloud, so at least all of that is saved. I'll change my passwords, though, and check the settings to make sure that I've got a second level of security turned on."

Sue and Jennifer started for the door, but Mogi was still cursing himself for missing such an obvious place to look. Stupid!

"I'm going to stay here and think about things," he said. "I'm not a real intern, anyway. Go ahead and take the key back. If I leave, I'll close the padlock and walk back to the dorm."

The girls agreed and Mogi found himself alone in the room. He closed the door and sat on the side of the bed.

Somebody had been on the other side of that basement door. Ghosts don't cough, and they don't sneeze, either.

Mogi sat down at the computer, logged in under Sue's name, and opened a new document.

For the next hour, he listed everything he had done and learned since coming to the Castañeda, including a short version of the Harvey Girls history, the artifacts they had found in the hotel, the items in the footlocker, what the letters and newspapers said, and what little he knew of Margaret Simpson—her history, her role at the Castañeda, and her suicide.

He felt a headache coming on. It was just too much, too many little pieces of unrelated information, but he couldn't give up. If he didn't at least get everything into some form that was easy to remember, he'd never be able to make sense of it.

Sorting things as he typed, he created five categories of facts and questions:

- Before the bank robbery: Margaret Simpson started working as a Harvey Girl at a hotel in Williams, Arizona, in 1926. Where was she born, where did she grow up, what happened to her family? She was married, her husband died, she hired on with the Castañeda in 1935 as senior girl. Why did she never have children?

- The day of the robbery: the events in the bank, the description of the men. Who were they, where did they come from, why didn't they cover their faces? Why didn't it matter if people saw that they were twins? How did they vanish into thin air? What happened to the money, guns, bag, etc.?

- Margaret Simpson and the robbery: The bank was two blocks from the hotel. It was noon, so she was working and couldn't have participated in the robbery. Did she know that it was going to happen? Was she involved, or did she see something? Did the bills in the Bible come from the bank? How did she end up with several hundred-dollar bills and the two watches? Suppose she was involved: Did she hide the money? Did she spend it? How much was taken anyway? If she did hide it, it could still be where she put it. How could someone find it?

- After the robbery: What was happening in May of 1945? What happened to make Margaret commit suicide? She paid for the funeral and the grave marker. Why? Did the date of her death, May 7, have any special meaning? Did the bank robbers come back? If so, was it to get the money? To reward her? To threaten her? Were they involved in her death?

- Leftover questions: Who was in the basement? Were they looking for the money? Who took the footlocker and why? The letters—how were they connected? Why so few? When were they received? Did Margaret reply? Who were *Wyatt* and *Doc*? Were they relatives? Friends? Children of friends? Acquaintances? Soldiers she'd met at the Castañeda?

Mogi's eyes grew heavy and he squirmed, trying to keep his body upright. None of this had helped his headache. College life wasn't exactly working out for him, even if it was his own fault. He missed his mom and dad making him go to bed, get up, have regular meals, and have some sort of order to every day. This wandering around and being in charge of yourself was hard work.

When he finally stopped thinking of things to write down, Mogi printed a copy, turned the computer off, staggered to the bed across the room, and fell across it, asleep in moments.

———

"Are you asleep again? Good grief! Get a grip, kid."

Jennifer and Sue had come back from class bringing a sack of hamburgers and a carrying tray with three drinks.

Jennifer cleared space on the table to spread out the food.

Mogi blinked several times, rolled over, and checked the time on his phone. It was almost one o'clock. He'd been out for two hours.

"You'll want to look at this," Jennifer said, tossing him a page of the Town Reporter. "It's the latest from our favorite journalist. We picked it up at the Student Union."

The Town Reporter
Bank Robbery Mystery Deepens
Monday, July 17—The legend of the robbery of the Las Vegas State Bank in 1943 is taking new

and different turns. The foot-locker found by the Castañeda's historical research team last month has been stolen.

The locker has been under close scrutiny after producing exciting new clues last week in solving the mystery of the robbery. The two pocket watches used in the crime, newspapers containing articles about the crime, and several one-hundred-dollar bills were all found hidden in the footlocker. The bills were the same denomination as the money stolen from the bank. One-hundred-dollar bills were unusual in 1943, so this is no coin-cidence.

Those items proved that its owner, Margaret Simpson, a long-time Harvey Girl at the Castañeda, was intimately involved in the robbery and was probably even the leader of the gang.

But now, with the theft of the footlocker, a new theory has arisen in the mind of this inves-tigator: Perhaps Margaret Simpson was not the ringleader but an innocent witness to the crime. The dastardly criminals may have threatened her into not revealing their identities. The money found in the Bible's leather cover may have been hush money, her silence purchased for a few bills from the bank's vault.

Who stole the footlocker? Seventy-five-years-plus after the robbery, is there still someone, some long-time confidant of the robbers, who has come back to claim the forgotten money?

The investigation continues, and this newspaper will keep readers fully informed.

CHAPTER 12

"What a jerk!" Mogi said, tearing the newspaper in two.

"Hey, that was our only copy!" Jennifer said

"Uh…whoops, sorry. I'll get us another one."

"Yes, I think you will."

"Anyway," Mogi began again, "he had her as the bank robber last week, then had her being the leader of the gang. Now he writes that she was a witness to something and was paid to keep everything a secret. He's an idiot. And he's still using the word *dastardly*! Does the guy not own a thesaurus?

"Wait a minute, I didn't think anybody knew the footlocker was stolen. How'd he know that?"

"Well, the class knew," Jennifer said, thinking about that morning. "There was a big discussion about who might have taken it and what might happen to it. Throw in Facebook, texting, and Twitter feeds and the whole world could have known about it before lunch."

"So Gabriel Sanchez finds out, writes his article, has it printed, and then distributes it by noon? I have to admire the guy for organization and hustle."

"By the way," Jennifer said, "Dr. Sanford told us that the history department has been swamped with emails and texts about the footlocker and the letters. They had to take their website down for a day to move it to another server that could handle the load. Colonel Hurley was right about people going nuts over this."

"Well, I'm glad somebody's having a good time with the letters," Mogi said, reaching for his backpack. He took out a handful of pages and spread them across the mattress.

"I went through the first five letters, marking everything I thought could possibly reveal anything. These are the next five. I'm still not finding any hidden secrets or anything. Wyatt tells it like it was, which was terrible, but he doesn't say a whole lot more."

Sue and Jennifer looked at the pages as he taped them on the wall.

Dear Mrs. Margaret Simpson:

Doc and I got to march down the streets of Paris! It was quite a sight for me and my older cousin. Didn't have to skip to stay in step

with everybody else and saluted at the right
time. It felt mighty good and I was proud. The
Paris people are crazy in love with all of us.
Then we got drunk. I vomited in the back of
the truck that I was riding in and everybody
got mad at me even though they were as drunk
as I was. I think we're moving north now but
I can't tell you where. They don't even tell me.
The weather is going to turn against us and
nobody has cold weather gear. It is already
getting cold at night. But we marched in
Paris!

    Wyatt and Doc.

    Dear Mrs. Margaret Simpson:
    We've moved through some pretty big
towns and a lot of them have been bombed by
our planes. Boy those bombs do a lot of
damage. Some of the towns had big buildings
like churches and castles, all made out of
stone, and the bombs made a pile of rubble out
of them. Where the towns have been bombed,
the people who survived don't have anywhere
to go. That leaves long lines of people along the
road and big groups standing on all the street
corners. Nothing to eat. Nowhere to go. Lots
of kids. We throw our ration chocolate to

them and boy do they fight over the candy. Lots of old people too, I guess, because all the young men had to join the army and go to fight. I hate seeing the poor people. I expect they're starving. Come winter, times will be hard.

Wyatt and Doc.

Dear Mrs. Margaret Simpson:

We're in the north country and it's cold and I'm cold all the time like everybody else. We must be pretty far north, a lot farther north than home, making it cold cold cold. There's ice on everything in the morning. The days are pretty dark and dreary with cloud cover. The cold makes my loneliness worse. I'm tired of this war and I'm tired of moving all the time and chasing other soldiers and I'm tired of digging foxholes and tired of sleeping in foxholes. I might go into the foxhole digging business after the war, ha ha, because I'm getting so good at it. Sometimes it's plain dirt where they planted crops but sometimes we are in trees and that's worse because of all the roots. I wish I was home. My older cousin, Doc, is getting down like he used to when we were kids and I try to brighten him up but everybody's tired and gruff. It would be beautiful country if we could stop and settle for a while and not have to watch the lines of the poor hungries and the surrendering troops. I don't normally complain about surrendering troops but we stop pretty often and Doc and I are always ordered to set up barbed wire fences to make compounds for them to stay captured in. I kind of thought we should shoot them all but I guess that's kind of cruel. I wouldn't want them shooting me if I was captured so I guess I'll keep putting up wire.

Wyatt and Doc.

Dear Mrs. Margaret Simpson:

I killed a man today and I wish I hadn't done it. I've killed before but never so close. I was going through a building to see if it was empty and there was a German soldier coming down a stairway just as I saw him and I shot him in the chest but he didn't die right away. He moved his hand inside his jacket and I shot him again, thinking that he was going for a pistol or something. He was reaching for a picture of his girlfriend. His helmet came off and he wasn't as old as I am. Just a kid. It doesn't seem right that he had to die. It doesn't seem right that I had to kill him. Maybe he was coming down the stairway to surrender but I don't know and I did what I was trained to do which is to shoot first. I wasn't that surprised by him, just doing my job and making sure that it was me that lived. I worry about it though. I wish you were here to talk to.

Wyatt and Doc.

Dear Mrs. Margaret Simpson:

Not many people make friends in this army. My unit's been pretty shot up so we get replacements, which is what Doc and I were in the first place so I can understand what it is like for them. But you don't make friends with any of them because you know that most of them are going to die. I'm an old hand at this war business so I keep working my system of staying alive and out of the sights of some Jerry's rifle. But I wish I had a friend or two. It gets lonesome here with nobody to talk to and Doc's not really good at it so we don't.

Wyatt and Doc.

"What's it like to kill someone?" Jennifer asked. "Even in a war, pointing a rifle at someone, pulling the trigger, and watching them die must have been tough on soldiers."

"I read a story once about the airmen in the bombers that dropped thousands of tons of bombs on German cities," Sue said. "They killed an uncountable number of people on their raids but they talked about never feeling it, never comprehending the loss of life because they were flying so high that all they saw was smoke and fire.

"Watching someone die right in front of you must have been way different."

Mogi nodded his head in agreement. "Even eighty years later, I feel sorry for Wyatt. Cold, no friends, nobody to talk to. At least he could write to Margaret. I really wish we knew the relationship between the two guys and Margaret. I'm sure she hurt for them, maybe more for Wyatt than Doc, but I bet she saw a million soldiers pass through the train depot and restaurant. A million soldiers saw her. What was it that made these two guys special?

"I wonder if she wrote them back and what she said if she did."

Jennifer turned and walked to the window. Something about the letters had made her wonder why Wyatt seemed so distant with his words but so close with his feelings.

"Did your grandparents fight in World War II?" Sue asked.

"I don't know about my dad's dad—I've never

thought to ask him," Mogi replied. "But my mom's dad was a veteran. All I know about him is that he fought in Europe."

"He never talked about it?"

Mogi shrugged. "I don't remember that he ever said anything to anybody."

"I know a little more," Jennifer said. "You were still in elementary school when he died. A week or two after the funeral, I talked to Mom. Because of his cancer, Grandpa was pretty much drugged all the time, but one night, he was lying on the couch and started talking about the war. Mom listened for more than an hour about what he did, where he went, and what it was like.

"He turned twenty years old a month after he landed on Omaha Beach in July 1944. He had used a welding machine during the summers in high school, so the recruiter put him in a combat engineering company that was responsible for repairing the roads, bridges, railroad tracks, and airfields that the German army had damaged or destroyed as they retreated, or else had been bombed by Allied planes.

"He said it was really hard work and they had to invent fixes to all sorts of problems right on the spot. They carried truckloads of stuff with them, like wood beams, steel girders, inflatable rafts, boats, train rails, bulldozers, road graders, and cranes, plus every kind of tool possible. They worked crazy hours, sometimes all day and all night, repairing things so that when the troops got to where they were, they could keep going.

"But it meant that his company was out in front a

lot, sometimes working while the Germans were still shooting at them. The army had to send infantry to fight them off so the engineers could get their jobs done."

"Did he ever get shot at or wounded?" Mogi asked.

"He said that a number of his company were wounded, but most of them were hurt by exploding land mines or booby-traps rather than bullets. When they worked in villages clearing roads, he saw a lot of dead civilians and sometimes had to help get their bodies out of the way."

"All that and he was only twenty?" Sue said. "I'm twenty, and I can't see myself doing anything in a war! Did he kill anybody? You know, like Wyatt did?"

"I don't remember Mom saying anything about him killing anyone. She took it pretty hard that Grandpa had lived so long with all those memories without telling anybody. She guessed that he was still haunted by what he had seen and experienced."

CHAPTER 13

"Okay. We've got things to do," Jennifer said. It was the next day and the three friends were in their usual positions in the team room at the hotel. They all hoped it was going to be a better day than Monday. They needed to make progress on the reunion activities.

"Thanks to our thief, we have to change the exhibit," she said. "The footlocker was going to be the center of attention. As much publicity as it's generated, I figured it would be our main draw. Now people are going to ask about it all day and we'll have to tell them that we don't have it. Can you generate a sign that says it was stolen?" she asked Mogi.

"Sure, no problem."

"Thank you. Let me review what's supposed to happen and when, and you two tell me if I've missed anything.

"We're one week and four days from the owner opening the doors to the hotel and letting the whole town walk through. Our Harvey Girl reunion has the formal dining room reserved while the exhibit, posters, and stuff are in the front entryway. The regular crowd won't be allowed into the dining room and kitchen until after we've finished and they've cleaned up. The owner is responsible for the signs that keep everybody out.

"Our Harvey Girl count is at nineteen, since the lady from Tennessee dropped out. The Plaza Restaurant downtown is catering the lunch, which they'll serve from the Castañeda's kitchen, and is also bringing several large platters of snacks that will be set on the lobby counter. The cake will be ready to pick up Saturday morning at nine, Dr. Sanford is picking it up. The flowers will be delivered by eight, and the florist will set everything up for us.

"The construction crew will place the portable toilets on Friday, somewhere on the north end of the yard next to the sidewalk so the smell will be away from everybody. Did you know that they make portable toilets that can accommodate wheelchairs? They're twice as big as the regular ones, with little ramps and everything.

"Anyway, the arts and crafts and food vendors will probably be here by seven and are bringing their own tents and tables and stuff, so we're okay there. Four of the food vendors requested power, so the construction guys are running plugs from the construction trailer.

"We can use all next week to work with the organizations that are setting up displays in the lobby. I've asked them all to set up on Friday so everything will be ready Saturday morning. Mogi has offered to make signs for everyone so they'll all look uniform, which will make the room pretty sharp looking.

"The Harvey Girls' banquet starts at eleven. They'll eat first, then the owner will give his welcome and an overview of the building and its history. Dr. Sanford will give a talk about the work the assessment team has done, a lady from the New Mexico History Museum will give a slide show on the history of Fred Harvey, and then a guy from the governor's office will recognize all the Harvey Girls with certificates. After that, the dining room and kitchen will be open until four o'clock. We should all be out by six. The owner has a crew who'll do the cleanup."

Jennifer paused, thought for a moment, and then said, "I think that's it."

"You've done a lot of work," Sue said.

"We've all done a lot of work," Jennifer said. "Summer's almost gone."

Sue went back to Dr. Sanford's office to see if her keys were ready while Mogi and Jennifer started sorting through the artifacts strewn around the room.

"I really wish we had that quilt," Jennifer said with a sigh. "You know that big open space on the west wall? That's where I was going to put it. The table with the footlocker and its stuff was going to sit directly in front of it, and we'd set the bed and night-stand on the right. On the other side, we were going to have a separate table for the artifacts, with your posters behind it. It was going to be really nice."

"The display will still be nice," Mogi said, "just a little smaller."

———

An hour later, Sue appeared at the door. "Guess what?" she said, holding up a set of keys. "Got 'em back!"

"Woohoo!" Mogi shouted. "Tunnels! We're gonna find some tunnels!"

"Hey, wait a minute," Jennifer said. "We're in the middle of work here."

"Aw, come on," he said. "We've got the rest of the week, and you've already got everything planned anyway. Besides, if we go do our exploring now, we can get it over with and I won't be bugging you anymore. Come on, let's go!"

Jennifer looked at Sue. "Aren't you the one who said that students were forbidden to go into the basement?"

Sue gave a small smile and shrugged. "True. But we're on a quest here, trying to save the reputation of a Harvey Girl, and we've already broken the rules for being in the building at night."

"I have an idea," Jennifer said, irritated by her brother. "Why don't you go find the tunnels while Sue and I stay and do the real work? You can come back and let us know what you found."

Mogi smiled. "That won't work. Who's going to protect me if I'm attacked by zombies?"

Jennifer rolled her eyes and gave up.

They grabbed three flashlights and made their way to the basement.

———

The threesome looked closely at the floor as they came down the wooden stairs from the kitchen, through the door where they had listened to the not-a-ghost breathing a few days before. The dusty concrete was covered with shoe prints—the waffle soles of the construction crew's work boots and prints from several types of sneakers favored by the assessment team. But there was also a different print—a man's shoe with a slick sole and rubber heel.

The basement spanned the width of the hotel's center section but stretched only from the north wall to the far side of the kitchen, about halfway down the wing. After that, the utility pipes ran through a crawl-space. Strings of construction lights had been nailed to the beams overhead and ran back and forth over the space, giving good light to most of the basement but leaving shadows near the walls.

The room was crowded with pipes: large insulated steam pipes branching into smaller pipes that then spread out to feed the radiators, other small pipes that served as electrical conduits, water lines, or vent pipes, gas pipes for the kitchen, and heavy-looking black pipes that took the hotel's wastes out to the sewer. Several disconnected sections of insulated pipe were stacked in the middle.

Mogi guessed that they were the sources of asbestos.

When he saw broken pieces of brick and stone on the floor and chip marks in the basement wall, he reached high overhead in a touchdown signal. "Yes! This confirms that the pounding we heard was real and that it wasn't a ghost. Whoever it is, he's real, and he's looking for something."

"If Margaret was left with a bag stuffed with money and clothes—maybe even the pistols— this would probably have been the best place to hide it," Sue said. "I bet nobody came down here very often."

"That would be my first choice," Mogi said. "Even with a room to herself, she was living among two dozen other women. It would have been impossible to hide a big bag in her room."

After scanning the perimeter of the room and following the crowded weave of pipes, they found the tunnel entrance easily. It was an arched passageway with a concrete floor and curved bricked ceiling, with *North Utility Tunnel* painted across the entrance. Pipes coming out of the tunnel hung from steel rods drilled into the ceiling, with electrical conduits hanging below. Even though there were fewer pipes, the curving walls and ceiling made it more crowded than the basement and made the three hunch over to walk.

"This has got to be how our mystery man got into the basement," Mogi said. "Let's go."

Fifty feet down the passageway, an ache began developing between his shoulders. Stooping over to be four feet tall was a killer, and the two girls didn't have it much better. It was also tough stepping around a century's worth of rat and mouse poop, fallen bits of insulation, dirt, grime, puddles from leaks in the ceiling, old blankets, scattered beer cans, and a pillow or two. The tunnel smelled like a swamp.

Mogi couldn't judge the distance very well, but if the steam plant was fifty yards north of the hotel, then the tunnel should have been about a hundred fifty feet long, or about a hundred steps. He was surprised when, not more than thirty steps from the entrance, another tunnel showed up on the left, with a large pipe from the north tunnel curving into it.

"What in the world is this?" he asked.

"Oh, I know," Sue said. "I bet it's the tunnel that takes steam and utilities to the annex across the street, which was a dorm for the Harvey Girls. It was built after the hotel and depot, so they must have added another tunnel to hold the new pipes for heating it. I don't have a key to the building since it's not part of our assessment. Let's hope we don't run across any locked doors."

"Look," Jennifer said, pointing her flashlight at the floor. A familiar set of shoe prints led into the left tunnel. "Our mystery guy went this way too."

They headed into the new tunnel. It wasn't as jammed with pipes or equipment, and Mogi could almost stand up in it. How far across the street was the annex? Maybe a hundred feet at most, Mogi thought, so maybe they were already past the curb?

He wished there were windows or skylights to give them more light. With only three flashlight beams to illuminate the space, the tunnel was as oppressive as a mineshaft.

All three explorers were aching from being hunched over when they hit a larger opening at the end, where the pipes suddenly curved up toward a metal grate. A ladder anchored to the wall led up to a square-hinged door in the grate.

The trio stood up, stretched their backs, and cautiously climbed the ladder.

CHAPTER 14

They each carefully stepped from the last metal rung up through the trapdoor opening to find themselves in the building's utility room. The large steam pipe from the tunnel had turned upward and divided into smaller pipes that disappeared into the floor or kept going until they branched into the ceiling. The water pipes split off as well, and the conduit bent over to the wall to join the bottom of a modern electrical panel.

An open doorway led from the room into a hallway extending from the back of the building to the front of a stairway on their right. Somewhere above them, there must have been windows letting in natural light. They followed the hallway to the bottom of the stairs, stepping over heaps of broken boards, doors, shelves, glass, floor tile, wallboard, and light fixtures, all covered in a thick blanket of dust and rotted leaves. The smell was so bad that they covered their noses with their sleeves.

A once-elegant stairway, still with its curved banister, led up the center of a two-story atrium to a circling walkway of empty doorways. High above, daylight barely came through a skylight crusted over with leaves and dirt.

"I haven't been here before," Sue said as she swept her eyes around. "I read in some book that this is the Rawlins Building. The rooms upstairs were bedrooms, each with beds for two or four Harvey Girls. There's one bathroom. Downstairs, there are two or three bedrooms plus a second bathroom, a kitchen, and a dining room. The whole place housed two dozen women and a house mother.

"In later life, the building was converted into offices. Looking at all the filth on the floor, it must have been some time ago."

The trio toured every corner of every room, appalled at the mess and damage but curious to see what home was like for the Harvey Girls. Young and innocent, typically from places far from New Mexico, they worked hard in a land that wasn't even a state until fourteen years after the Castañeda was built. The dormitory and hotel were their only refuge in what must have seemed like a stark and primitive land.

The entrance to the two-story building consisted of a single door. On each side, the walls had been removed and large floor-to-ceiling panes of glass were added to give the building a glass front from one side of the room to the other. When the building was abandoned, the glass panes had been removed and

replaced with plywood. The loss of light was significant, and the unpainted plywood panels were now
warped, splintered, and stained, making the downstairs, even more than its cluttered floor, feel worn
out, cheap, and ugly.

"This must have been a madhouse," Jennifer said as
they climbed the stairs to check out the upstairs
rooms.

"Only two bathrooms? Are you kidding? That was
back in the day when they had curling irons and flat-
tening irons and clothes irons and ironing boards.
Notice, by the way, that there are no closets."

Sue laughed. "That's where the footlockers came
in. One per girl, maybe a dresser, and the suitcase
they brought with them. That was it for storage."

"Were they paid much?" Mogi asked. "You'd have
to give me a ton of money to live in a place like this,
and I'm not talking about sharing it with a roommate.
Our dorm rooms are bigger than what I'm looking at."

"They earned about $30 a month," Sue said. "They
did get some perks, like free train travel every six
months to anywhere the Santa Fe railroad went, but I
think the big compensation was being part of a highly
respected, first-class business, plus a closeness to the
others that bonded them like a family. When Fred
Harvey started, this was the last frontier of America,
and I bet every girl was scared to death."

The upper bathroom was straight out of a horror
movie. Without water in the taps, every toilet, sink,
and drain was a straight pipe into the town sewer
system. The stench made them gag.

Mogi and Sue went into a bedroom overlooking the street while Jennifer wandered back downstairs. Directly across the street was the long sidewalk with cottonwood trees. They stood at the window taking in the view, remarking at how cramped the building must have felt, when they heard a faint noise that gradually grew louder.

Someone was crying.

Mogi immediately launched himself downstairs, leaping until he was at the bottom, and followed the sound through the doorway on his left.

Jennifer knelt on the floor among the trash, weeping as if tragedy had just struck.

"What?" he said, kneeling next to her. "Are you hurt? What happened?"

Jennifer couldn't answer, her throat thick with misery.

Sue rushed in, and together, they helped Jennifer up and walked her out of the room. As soon as she stepped over the threshold, her voice returned. "Oh my God! Did you feel the sadness?"

After calming down a bit, Jennifer told them how she had gone into the room, grown dizzy, and then felt herself drop to the floor. A wave of misery and sadness enveloped her until she could do nothing but burst into tears.

Sue looked back at the room. "It's at the bottom of the stairs, right on the hallway to the back door. This would have been the house mother's room. This is where Margaret Simpson lived."

The realization shook them all, and it took a few

minutes of sitting on the steps for Jennifer to regain her composure.

"Well," Sue finally said, "I think we've had enough for today. Everybody okay with going back?"

Jennifer and Mogi nodded, and they all walked toward the utility room they'd come in through.

Mogi suddenly stopped.

There was another room, on the inside of the hallway to the left of the utility room. He hadn't noticed it when they turned right into the hallway.

The room had a door, and the door was shut.

The three fell to a complete and uneasy silence. There was no door on any of the other rooms. Moving to the door as silently as possible, they listened for a long time and heard nothing. Mogi slowly turned the doorknob and then opened it with a swift movement.

The room was the same size as the others, but the thick layer of grunge on the floor had been cleared away. In the middle of the far wall was an object that was growing more mysterious every time they encountered it.

The footlocker.

It was open, and most of the items that had been inside were piled beside it on the floor.

The locker itself was a surprise, but they were stunned by what they found on the walls. All around the room, thumbtacked to every surface, were papers from the locker: the newspapers, the receipts, the letters—all spread out like someone was trying to solve a mystery.

Mogi was speechless. What in the world! He slowly stepped around the room, examining each piece, staring as if he hadn't seen them before. He, of course, remembered everything, which was why he was so puzzled. All the items had already been viewed, recorded, and photographed, and many had been published. Any hint of secrets they might have contained would have long since been found and made public.

"I don't understand," Jennifer said, standing in the center of the room, as puzzled as her brother was.

"Putting everything up this way is like what they do in the cop shows when they're tracking information about criminals. Why is all of this here?"

Sue was silent but wide-eyed. "Okay, this is officially weird. Whoever it is is obviously looking for something he thinks everybody else has missed."

"But he still doesn't know what, does he?" Mogi said slowly. "He's as mystified as we are."

Whoever it was, it had to be the not-a-ghost in the basement and was obviously the one who had stolen the footlocker. Ever since the money was found in the Bible, Mogi had always considered the person to be one step ahead of them. But this...this level of detailed examination made it look like the not-a-ghost didn't have a clue where to go next. He had hit a dead end.

"Well, I don't know why he put everything on the walls," Mogi said after taking a deep breath, "but I'm not about to leave it. Let's get this stuff back in the footlocker and get out of here."

With Sue keeping watch, Mogi and Jennifer

hurriedly gathered the papers from the walls and layered them in the locker, added the rest of the contents, and then packed it all down with the quilt on top. Then they started struggling to carry it into the utility room.

"Wait a minute," Mogi said. "Why don't we just carry it outside? We could go out the back door and go across the street."

"I don't have a key, remember?" Sue said. "We could unlock it from the inside, but I wouldn't be able to lock it from the outside. Besides, we're not even supposed to be in this building. If we're seen, some-body's going to think we broke in or something."

"Okay, okay," Mogi said, lowering his lanky frame through the trapdoor with a grunt. When he was halfway down the ladder, he reached up to catch the end of the locker as Jennifer and Sue lowered it down.

If the trip through the tunnel had hurt the first time, the second time was torture. They manhandled, shoved, balanced, turned, dragged, upended, and otherwise carried the footlocker as they negotiated the pipes, conduits, and littered floor.

In spite of the pain, though, they sometimes erupted into laughter. They felt like pirates escaping with a stolen chest, hurrying to hide their booty before being discovered by the deranged captain of their ship.

CHAPTER 15

As they expected, The Town Reporter published a new issue the next day.

The Town Reporter
New Developments in Las Vegas Legend

Wednesday, July 19—In the continuing investigation into the robbery committed at the Las Vegas State Bank in 1943, a major development has occurred: The footlocker stolen a few days ago that belonged to Margaret Simpson, possibly the ringleader of the gang, has been found in the auxiliary building across the street from the Castañeda Hotel.

The auxiliary, known as the Rawlins Building, served as the dormitory for the hotel's Harvey Girls during the war years.

Through an intensive investigation over the last few weeks, Margaret Simpson has been identified as the person responsible for planning the robbery of the Las Vegas State Bank on October 16, 1943.

Evidence includes the watches used by the two men who committed the robbery, seven incriminating newspaper articles, and several one-hundred-dollar bills found hidden in a family Bible. These show without a doubt that Margaret Simpson was into the crime up to her neck.

The investigation continues into who the two bandits were, what their relationship to Simpson was, and what happened to the large amount of money that was stolen. Is it hidden in the Castañeda? The Rawlins Building? Or was it long ago destroyed to protect the thieves?

This reporter continues to be

at the forefront of searching for
more clues. As always, readers
will be informed of progress at
every point along the way.

CHAPTER 16

Jennifer was right—a lot of work remained to be done, and with the classwork finished, the team members who had volunteered to help with the display drifted away.

All the work now fell to Sue, Jennifer, and Mogi.

But Mogi worked with only half the dedication he usually did. He was busy thinking about other things.

He hadn't made any headway with the list he'd created on Sue's computer, he'd had no insights in determining whether the letters contained hints of Margaret Simpson's situation, he couldn't help but be influenced by Gabriel Sanchez's terrible articles— what if she had planned the robbery?—and he couldn't imagine what it was like to fight in a war.

That was a surprising result of the letters—his curiosity about the war. In his history classes in middle school, the teachers talked mostly about the American Revolution and the Civil War. If it weren't for HBO, PBS, and some of the movies he'd watched, he wouldn't know anything about World War II. He also had heard various facts about the war but didn't know how everything fit together.

For the United States, the official war lasted from the attack on Pearl Harbor in 1941 to the surrender of Japan in 1945, and involved some sixteen million American soldiers, airmen, sailors, and others. It severely impacted the entire nation and most of the world, yet he couldn't draw maps of any of the other countries that were heavily involved, nor could he describe the sequence of what had happened when. He knew some of the countries in Europe by name but none of the islands in the Pacific. He knew Hitler was the bad guy in Europe but didn't understand how Russia first fought with Germany but then fought against Germany. He knew squat about Italy's role, which was also first with Germany and then against Germany. He had seen unbelievably horrible pictures of concentration camps but didn't really understand the Holocaust or what had led up to it.

He couldn't even imagine what Wyatt was talking about when he described soldiers digging foxholes. Foxholes?

They really dug holes in the ground and slept in them? In the snow? Why would they do that? Did Grandpa sleep in foxholes? When he wrote his V-mail letters home to Grandma, did he tell her about them? How would she have reacted if he'd told her that he killed someone?

———

It was Thursday, nine days before the reunion, that disaster struck.

After working all afternoon and having a supper of the unendingly delicious chicken enchiladas at Mike's Café, Mogi went back to his room and found it in shambles.

The mattress had been yanked off the bedframe, the sheets torn off, and the dresser drawers dumped out, his clothing strewn all over. His laptop had been thrown to the floor, shattering the screen. The walls where Wyatt's letters had been taped up were barren. Mogi went ballistic. He yelled, kicked the mattress, punched his pillow.

His computer! And the files on his computer—what would he do now?

For the first time, he felt that Margaret Simpson's mystery was getting personal.

He called Jennifer, who called Sue, who called Dr. Sanford. They all came immediately. Dr. Sanford was as angry as the rest of them. If university students were responsible for this, she wasn't about to let them get away with it.

She immediately began making calls to administrators.

The campus police couldn't determine who had done it. The door lock had new scratch marks, meaning it had been picked, but they could find no other clues. There were few other students staying in the dorm for the summer, so there were no witnesses.

The mess was declared a crime scene, and Mogi was given new bedding and the key to a different room nearby. University security people took Mogi's laptop to have the IT department try to recover the files. That was the best anyone could do.

When asked if they could identify a likely suspect, Mogi, Sue, and Jennifer agreed not to implicate Gabriel Sanchez. Being angry and ranting about him was one thing, but blurting out his name without proof was another. It would only make the situation worse, and it might get him blamed for something he didn't do.

The three decided, instead, to pay a visit to the fine reporter.

After breakfast the next morning, it was simple enough to find Sanchez's address, and they were soon ringing his doorbell. When Sanchez answered the door, they were shocked to see that his face was bruised, his lips bloody, and one eye swollen.

"I expected you to show up someday," he said and led them down a stairway into the basement, limping as he did.

Mogi was primed for confrontation. "You fall down the stairs after tossing my room? Tripped in the parking lot, huh? What's the big idea? What were you looking for?"

"Whoa!" Sanchez said, sitting down in an office chair and cupping his head in his hand. "Tell me what you think I did before you take my head off, okay?"

Jennifer described Mogi's room.

"Not me," Sanchez said. "Sorry, but your room wasn't the only thing that got tossed yesterday."

"How about the letters? I did a lot of work on those letters. I want them back!" Mogi yelled.

Sanchez took an ice pack from his desk and held it over his swollen eye. "You need the letters to send to Mommy or something?"

"Wait, wait, wait," Jennifer said, seeing that anger and insult were taking over. "You mind if we sit down?"

"Go right ahead. Grab the folding chairs over there."

The basement was a mess, with overflowing book-shelves, a folding table covered with piles of paper, a shabby couch pushed up against the wall, and two cluttered desks. A large computer monitor sat on one of the desks with a laptop in front of it. Sunlight came in through a few dirty windows while the well-worn carpet gave off an ancient smell.

"Okay," Jennifer said. "I met you when you came to look at the footlocker. From the time you did that, you've written articles for The Town Reporter dealing with Margaret Simpson and the Las Vegas robbery."

"You are correct," he responded. "And if you'd speak softer, I'd appreciate it. I've got a little headache from having my head bounced on the floor."

"I was there for your little footlocker exposé as well," Sue said, jumping into the conversation. "You stole the keys to the building, stole the footlocker, took it over to the annex, and played your little inves-tigator game." Her voice grew louder as she went on. "And then you ran-sacked Mogi's room, destroyed his laptop, and stole the letters! Am I going too fast for you here?"

Sanchez raised both his hands in surrender. "Okay, I'm beginning to understand your visit. You can put your guns away. It wasn't me, not any of it. I write entertainment for The Town Reporter, but I don't do physical stuff. I do have an idea of who might be responsible, so let me tell you my story and you can see why I'm not crying all over myself for the great sins that you're laying at my feet.

"Three weeks ago, some guy comes up to me in the cafeteria. A guy with a big beard. You know I'm a student, right? A graduate student trying to get my master's in English so I can get the hell out of this town?

"Anyway, he says his name is Jack Grimes and that he's a treasure geek. Spends his time traveling to various places that have tales of lost treasure, hidden gold, stolen manuscripts. He likes finding mysteries and investigating them. Said he had a pretty good record of solving old puzzles, and it brings him enough money to stay in the business. He'd seen a TV report about the footlocker being found at the hotel and researched the legend of the bank robbery, and he's pretty sure he can make a connection between the robbery and the contents of the footlocker.

"Freelance treasure hunters are not very welcome in most places, which makes it hard to get local people to talk, so he makes me a proposition: He'll trade me information about the legend if I'll go through the footlocker and make sure that what he suspects is there is actually there. He promises it will be worth my while and then tells me that he'll provide more information if I keep writing articles about it.

"Well, I can always use material, and people like new interpretations of local legends and mysteries. I don't make anything from the papers I distribute around campus, but my online stuff brings me a few dollars from the advertising I include."

"You make up lies and then publish them like they're true," Sue said with an edge to her voice.

"I give a theatrical treatment to possible interpretations of truthful happenings and then present them for people's enjoyment."

"You lie to them."

"Pardon me," Sanchez looked at her with a you-can-shove-it expression, "but I am not a journalist when I write those articles. I am an entertainer. People know not to take The Reporter seriously. Jerry Springer had an abomination of a TV show for years, and it almost got him elected to Congress. How many people buy magazines at the grocery store featuring aliens, Bigfoot, and the Loch Ness monster? People love to be lied to, or at least they love to be presented with a possible version of the truth that's more interesting than the hard facts. Grow up."

"Okay, okay," Jennifer again interrupted the growing hostility. "Back to your story. What happened when you agreed to look at the footlocker?"

"He told me to look at the newspapers for articles about the robbery and then to take the cover off the Bible. After my first article about the robbery, which, by the way, had more hits than anything else I've ever done, he fed me more ideas about what might have happened, what the latest thinking was on Margaret Simpson's motives, etc. I was surprised at how often he came up with stuff, but it was fun telling the story as if I was the investigator."

He looked straight at Sue. "I've hardly had to lie at all."

Mogi had calmed down because Sanchez sounded truthful, and it was obvious he had been beaten up pretty badly. If what he was saying was true, he wasn't the not-a-ghost in the hotel basement, nor the guy who broke into his room, nor even the thief who took the footlocker.

"So Jack Grimes beat you up?" Jennifer asked.

"Yep. Showed up yesterday. Accused me of telling you where the footlocker was and was furious about losing it. I don't know why he thought I'd had any contact with you, but he may not be playing with a full deck, in my humble opinion."

"This guy," Jennifer asked, "how did he know about the money in the Bible? I guess he was right about there being a connection between Margaret Simpson and the robbery, but how did he know? Solving legends or not, working us against you is a pretty nasty way to find things out, so he must not know everything. Is he after the money from the robbery? Does he think it's still hidden someplace around here?"

"Oh, yeah, he wants the money, big time. I don't have a clue where Jack Grimes is from, but I'm betting he's no freelance treasure hunter. My guess is that he knows maybe half the story and is expecting the three of you to turn over some rock that will allow him to figure out all of it. He must think one of you is close to breaking the story, or at least close enough that he can now use force to get the rest of it."

They talked for a few minutes more, but it was clear to the three visitors that their host needed to lie down and take it easy for a while. As they stopped on the doorstep to thank him for being so open with them, Sanchez added a caution.

"Listen, Jack Grimes is bad news. He's not very tall, but he's solidly built. He must have grown up as a streetfighter. I think you should get your reunion over with and then get out of town. When he was beating the crap out of me, he was enjoying it, so you need to watch out, okay?"

CHAPTER 17

"Whatcha doin'?" It was Saturday. Mogi was sitting on the bed in his new room, propped up against his pillow, arms folded across his chest, his eyes open but not moving. His sister had just walked into the room.

"Thinking," he said.

"Getting it all figured out, huh?"

Mogi sighed. "I'm completely lost. My mind keeps looping through my categories. I can't identify one clear fact that ties everything together. First, there're the two men who did the robbery. Where did they come from, how did they know Margaret Simpson, how did they get the clothes, how did they know about the bank and the money, etc.

"Then there's Margaret. I don't know what she did —or didn't do—or why. When I think of her in 1945, I don't know if the money still existed and, if it did, if she was in control of it. I don't know whether the two men came back, and I don't even have a guess as to why she killed herself.

"Then there are the letters. Maybe they don't mean anything. Maybe Wyatt was just a lonely, scared soldier who had a simple way of saying things, who had met a pretty waitress. Maybe there's nothing to be revealed.

"And now there's a whole new character, Jack Grimes, who has obviously been jerking us around for weeks. He's looking for the money, which means he's convinced it exists. Why? What kind of insider information does he have that makes him convinced he's on the right track, and where did he get that info?

"If you throw in his getting violent with Gabriel Sanchez, things get darker. Is he going to come after us? Surely, he won't because we don't know anything. But, of course, he doesn't know that.

"I just can't find any connections that reveal a common thread."

Jennifer looked at the wall opposite his bed. All fourteen letters were taped on the wall, but none had any markings. "Did you reprint all of them?"

"I reprinted the first ten. The thief took the five that were all marked up and that I had taped on the wall, and the second five are in the team room. I had the last four already printed but hadn't put them up. I lost all the scribbling I did, so I thought I'd just tape everything to the wall. I've been staring at them at a distance and they all follow the same patterns: the same formal greeting, the same fake names, the same *older cousin* reference to Doc, the same sign-off with both names when only Wyatt writes the letters. The same stuff that doesn't tell us anything."

Jennifer walked over to the wall. The letters still made her curious and uncomfortable, but it was hard to pin down why. Fourteen letters. Why only fourteen? Did Wyatt write whenever he could, or did he write on a regular basis? Did he write whenever something happened?

She began to read the last four.

Dear Mrs. Margaret Simpson:

There are engineers that have to repair things in front of us so we can keep going forward. There was a bridge that the Krauts had blown up so that we couldn't use it to cross the river. The engineers pulled up next to it, put these really big inflatable pontoons in the water that reached all the way to the other side, and put a steel roadway right on top of them. Tada! They made a road that was strong enough to hold our tanks. They also fill in bomb holes in roads and landing strips. When Doc and I are at the very front of the unit, we get out of our half-tracks and get behind the tanks. When anybody shoots at us, we hide behind them until we have to spread out inside the town. That's when you need to know the tank driver so he doesn't go off and leave you.

Wyatt and Doc.

Dear Mrs. Margaret Simpson:

We had a bad fight and lost a lot of men. Damn Krauts! It took days which is why I haven't written. I've been in a foxhole for a couple of weeks, sleeping, eating my rations, covering the hole with branches and stuff that comes when the trees blow up from the mortars. I don't have much time to think straight because of all the bullets, rockets, shells, noise, stink, and the ground shaking. I stay scared all the time. I don't want to die, so I crawl into a corner of my foxhole, put my pack over my head, hold onto my chin strap with both hands, and pray that I'll see you again.

Doc, my older cousin, is always somewhere close and he just gets angry. I've known him to stand up in his foxhole and shout at the Krauts. But not for long—he's not stupid. The captain sent him out one night on a patrol to locate the German line. Almost got himself killed but he came back in one piece and brought a German pistol with him. That's okay because everybody picks up souvenirs. Now he'll want to do it again. I still like finding a tank to stay behind.

    Wyatt and Doc.

Dear Mrs. Margaret Simpson:

    I guess I didn't know that windmills were real. I remember pictures in books and I've seen postcards but Doc and I got a three-day pass to visit some of the sights around a nearby village and, what do you know, here are these buildings with giant fan blades! Pretty country, but it is flat flat flat. They need the windmills to pump the water back into the ocean. We're closer to a port on the ocean than we have been, so we're getting new supplies—tanks, trucks, artillery, ammunition, rations, and stuff like that. Then it is back to the front line. I hear bombers every night, so we must still be giving them hell. I guess they are bombing factories and airfields or such. It is still frigid and cold and there is lots of fog. Makes everything wet, especially in our foxholes. We finally got galoshes that fit over our boots. I hope they make a big difference because my feet stay soaked! I have to carry my spare socks inside my shirt to keep them dry until I swap them every night.

Wyatt and Doc.

Dear Mrs. Margaret Simpson:

Doc, my older cousin, and me are going to get some rest and relaxation! My unit's been on the front line for a while and the commanders are sending us into an area where there's no fighting. They have hot showers and kitchen food and there will be tents and cots for us to sleep on. Boy oh boy! There'll be other units but I hope they let us sleep. I want to sleep. I want Doc to get better, too. Somebody stole his galoshes and his feet got frostbite so he has trouble walking. He'll be all right as soon as he can dry out his boots and put on dry socks. Let us get off our feet, get out of the ice and snow, dry off someplace, and sleep sleep sleep. And eat. I hope they let us have as much food as we want. And a fire. I hope they keep a fire going so I can get warm. See, I told you not to worry about us. We just about got the Germans licked and we'll be together soon.

Wyatt and Doc.

. . .

We'll be together soon. Wyatt had never said that before, Jennifer thought. He and Margaret really must have had some kind of relationship.

She looked again at the greeting: *Dear Mrs. Margaret Simpson,* always with a colon at the end. She looked again at the sign-off: *Wyatt and Doc,* always with a period. The lettering for those parts of each letter was dark and clear, much clearer than the actual text of the letters. He must have sharpened his pencil before he wrote their names.

That's what he did! Jennifer realized. That's why it always looks the same! The lettering was much clearer than the body of each letter because Wyatt must have gotten all the paper forms for V-mail at one time. Then he wrote her name at the top and *Wyatt and Doc* at the bottom. He probably also wrote in her address on each form at the same time. Then, when he wanted to write a letter, he pulled out a form and wrote between her name and their names.

The greetings and sign-offs looked the same because he had a sharp point on his pencil when he printed them.

The inside text of each letter varied because he sometimes had a sharp pencil, but most of the time did not.

Why? Jennifer was still puzzled. Why would he write her name and their names all at once instead of each time he wrote? What difference would it make? It was like he was afraid he'd make a mistake. How in the world could he make a mistake writing her name and their names?

Then her eyes popped open.

Because he was afraid he might address her as something other than Margaret Simpson or that he might write their real names by mistake. That would mean she'd get a letter she would have to treat differently from the rest because…because…

Wait a minute. So what? She knew their names, and they knew her name. But what if someone else read the letters? Then they'd see the real names. So what? What difference would that make?

She gave a small gasp. It might have made a big difference.

Jennifer went to her room, returned with her laptop, and sat on the bed next to her brother. "Let's try a shot in the dark. Let's see if we can find out where Margaret Simpson lived. You remember Mom's password to that ancestor site she used to research our family?"

"Yup."

"Well, let's see what we can do." She went to the ancestor research website, turned the laptop toward Mogi so he could access it with their mother's username and password, then typed *Margaret Simpson* in the search bar, and waited.

"It wants a state," Jennifer said as a banner came up.

"Try Arizona," Mogi said. "We know she worked there, so maybe that's where she was born."

Jennifer typed in Arizona and waited. Another banner came up.

"It wants more of the name," she said.

"Maybe it had too many hits to list."

"Oh, here," Jennifer said with a huff, "you do it. I get irritated with this stuff."

Mogi moved the computer to his lap and added *Anne* as a middle name.

"Anne? You don't know that her middle name was Anne! What are you doing?"

"Well, it wanted something, so I gave it something. That will let it get past the question and go to work. When it comes back, it'll probably start with Margaret Anne Simpson and then list other names that aren't Margaret Anne Simpson. Then we'll see if any of the descriptions match our Margaret Simpson."

He was right. The search came back with many names.

"Oh, wait, wait, wait. Dummy!" Mogi suddenly said.

"I know her middle name. And her birthdate. It's in the Fred Harvey database."

Mogi reached over, grabbed a flash drive from the table, plugged it into the laptop, opened a new browser window, went to the Fred Harvey web page, gave it a password, and found the list of employees.

"Give me a minute here. We're looking for women hired in 1935 at the Castañeda. Okay, here it is: *Margaret Beth Simpson*. She was born January 6, 1908. She was twenty-seven when she started working at the Castañeda.

"Okay, now back to the ancestor site." He switched windows and typed in Margaret's name and birthdate.

Seven names came up, along with some other information. He and Jennifer read through the names.

"Well, that's not it. She must not have been born in Arizona."

"Wait, wait, wait," Jennifer said. "Go back."

"What? She's not listed."

"Stop! Let me look for a minute."

Jennifer read the screen. "There's her name, Margaret Beth Simpson, right there." She pointed. "And that's the right birthdate, but this information isn't about her. She's named as the mother on a birth certificate. That can't be right because we know she had no kids. But look, it happens again with the listing right below it."

Mogi kept looking. "It can't be our Margaret Beth Simpson. We know she never had kids."

"Didn't I just say that? Click there."

The image of a birth certificate came onto the screen.

They read it carefully. Then Mogi went back a page, clicked on the second entry, and brought up the second birth certificate in a separate window.

On both birth certificates, Margaret Beth Simpson was listed as the mother, while the father's name was blank.

"Warren Sam Simpson, Henry LeRoy Simpson. Who in the world are they?" Jennifer asked.

"Huh. We have two birth certificates listing

Margaret Beth Simpson as the mother, and the father unknown. Born in Arizona—"

"Oh my God!" Jennifer suddenly cried out. "Look at the birthdates! They're the same! She did have children! She had twins!"

That was the mistake Wyatt was afraid of making. He was afraid that in the middle of Europe, in the middle of the war, in the middle of combat, in the middle of all the cold, fear, and confusion, he might forget their plan and use Margaret's real name: *Mom.*

———

The next hour was like knocking down dominoes lined up in a row. Topple the first and the second falls, then the third, then the next.

Starting with Margaret Beth Simpson and her birthdate, Mogi and Jennifer ran through page after page on the ancestor site. Her parents, where they were born, where they lived, her own birth certificate—one thing after another popped up on the screen.

She was born on January 6, 1908, in Pining, Pennsylvania. Her mother was Elizabeth Elaine Farnum, married to Henry Pike Simpson. They were listed as missionaries for the Holy Reformed Dutch Church of Pining.

Looking through Wikipedia and other sources, Mogi zeroed in on the historic mission fields of the Holy Reformed Dutch Church. One of them was a Navajo outreach church outside Chinle, Arizona, the location of Canyon de Chelly, one of the Navajo Nation's most important historical sites.

"Wait a minute," Mogi said, clicking back to a different window. "Look at the birth certificates of the two boys. They were born in Williams, Arizona. That's on the other side of Flagstaff. That's where the train station is for the train that runs up to the Grand Canyon. It's probably less than two hundred miles from Chinle."

"If Margaret was a mother," Jennifer said, "and if her parents were missionaries connected to that church outside Canyon de Chelly, then I'm getting a bad feeling.

"Did you see how old Margaret was when she gave birth? They were born in 1924, so she was sixteen. Sixteen years old and pregnant. I'll bet you anything she wasn't married, and I'll bet you even more that her parents threw her out because of it. I would assume that being unmarried and pregnant was not tolerated by Holy Reformed Dutch Church missionaries, so they kicked her out of the house and out of the church and had nothing more to do with her."

"That's pretty harsh."

"Very harsh. But Chinle, Arizona, would have been a tough mission field. Imagine the parents working for years evangelizing the community, and then their daughter turns up pregnant. That would seriously erode the credibility they'd built up. It doesn't excuse at all their throwing their daughter out, but you can imagine the position they were in."

Jennifer leaned against the wall at the head of the bed.

"So, Margaret Simpson, age sixteen, is thrown out of her family and the church and maybe even shunned so badly that she can't stay in town. She's going to have the babies with no support from her parents, and it can't be in Chinle. I bet she chose Williams because she knew someone there, and it got her far away from Chinle and far away from where the deadbeat dad probably lived, whoever he was. Maybe some kind people helped her out, made arrangements.

"Maybe we shouldn't be too hard on her parents," Jennifer continued. "Maybe she chose to leave and they found her a friend in Williams. We don't know anything, really, but I'm betting someone reached out to her.

"Anyway, she has the babies, and sometime later, she finds a job at the Fred Harvey House in Williams. She thinks she's extraordinarily lucky because it's a great job with a great company. But she has to lie about her age, as well as about having children, meaning she has to leave the babies with a friend or another family, maybe the same friend who helped her get there. What else can she do? This is 1924 in the middle of nowhere. She's destitute with two babies to support."

"Okay," Mogi picked up the timeline, "so she's a Harvey Girl until 1931, when she marries one of the cooks, maybe bringing the kids into the home, maybe not. But she can't call them her children, so maybe she calls them nephews or whatever. Then, in 1935, her husband dies. Now she's on her own. She can't afford the house or apartment or whatever, and still has to support the two kids.

"She finds out there's an opening at the Castañeda for a senior girl, it pays a lot more than an ordinary Harvey Girl, and she gets room and board, which saves her a ton of money. In the middle of the Depression, she can't not go. She leaves the kids in Williams with whoever had kept them before, goes to the interview, and lies again that she doesn't have children. When they look up her Fred Harvey record, it will say that she has no kids, and she's far enough away from Williams so that nobody knows any different. Everything looks good and she's hired, and she sends money to help raise the boys.

"Now, in 1943, the twins are what—uh, 1943 minus 1924 is nineteen—the twins are nineteen, just the right age to join the army."

Jennifer's eyes popped open wide again. "That's why the letters are so odd! The boys were afraid that someone apart from Margaret would get ahold of them. If she was getting letters from someone whose names were Warren and Henry, with the last name Simpson, it could be guessed that they were her sons.

"That's why Margaret cut off the names and addresses of the V-mail!" Mogi exclaimed. "The military address would have used Wyatt's real name."

Jennifer nodded and continued. "So the twins use fake names in the letters and always refer to their mother as *Mrs. Margaret Simpson*. It's also why Wyatt makes it a point to so often refer to Doc as his *older cousin*, so no one will suspect that Wyatt and Doc are brothers."

Jennifer was still talking when she noticed that her brother wasn't listening. He was, in fact, staring off into space.

"What?" she said.

Mogi didn't reply, so she leaned back against a pillow and waited. After a few moments, he said, "Now, that was clever."

"What? What was clever?"

Mogi turned to look at her. "A troop train. I bet they were on a troop train. It came into the station close to noon and everybody got off for lunch, except for the twin brothers, who decided to skip lunch and rob a bank instead. They put on the new shirts and coveralls over their uniforms, went into the bank, had the clerk put the money in the bag, put everybody in the vault, and then took off the hats, shirts, and coveralls and stuffed them in the green bag with the money.

"Then, looking like soldiers again, they walked back to the train station and got back on the train. That's why nobody saw anyone strange walking away from the bank or in the area. The green bag was a duffel bag, an ordinary, everyday, army duffel bag. I bet there were always soldiers walking around with duffel bags. That's what makes it so clever! In 1943, with trainloads of soldiers coming in and going out every day, the two guys would have basically been invisible. No one would have noticed them getting off the train, walking around, and getting back on the train."

Jennifer sat for a moment, digesting the information.

"But wait a minute, where did they get the clothes and the guns? And what did they do with all their stuff afterward? And what about the money?"

"That's where Margaret Simpson comes in. She was behind it all, from the very beginning. She's the one who figured out the timing of the train, the bank procedures, the money schedule. She's the one who got the clothes and the guns, hid them someplace between the depot and the bank, where the twins could put on and take off everything, and then retrieved everything after the robbery. And she's the one who took the money and hid it.

"You found the keys to what the letters were telling us," he said, looking at Jennifer. "Now we need to know what happened to the boys, and I think we know someone who can find that out for us."

CHAPTER 18

After struggling to wait patiently all day Sunday, Mogi and Jennifer were at Colonel Hurley's office early Monday morning. He wasn't in, but the door was open, so they went inside.

The office was clean and orderly. Books were lined up on their shelves with no hint of dust. The framed photographs were of people in uniform, while a larger photo showed the colonel sitting next to a woman surrounded by three smiling teenagers. On the wall were two diplomas and several plaques, citations, and awards.

There were four chairs around a medium-sized round table.

At the other end of the room was a cluttered desk with a keyboard, monitor, and printer. Behind it, in the back corner, stood an American flag.

"Hey, it's the footlocker sleuths. What can I do for you?" the colonel said as he came through the door.

"Hello," Jennifer said. "I hope it's okay that we came in, the door was open."

"My door is always open, and you are welcome anytime," he said with a smile.

"We've made some discoveries," Mogi said, "and now we could use your help."

Colonel Hurley sat down behind his desk and motioned for them to pull two chairs over from the table.

"Tell me what you've got."

Mogi explained about going through the letters looking for clues. Jennifer told of her suspicion that they had been written to intentionally avoid mentioning names or relationships. Then they explained how they had used the ancestor site to track down Margaret Simpson and the births of her children and summed up what they thought Margaret's life had been like.

Mogi handed the colonel a printed sequence of who, where, and what he and Jennifer thought had happened.

"Well, I am impressed," Colonel Hurley said, reading through the paper. "That's some pretty good detective work. If either of you ever need a recommendation to get in the army, let me know. How can I help?"

"We'd like to know, for sure, if the two boys were in the army and, if so, what happened to them."

"Okey dokey. We can look that up." The colonel typed in his password and brought up a military database. Typing several entries, he looked at the results and then turned the screen so Mogi and Jennifer could see it.

Henry LeRoy Simpson
  Age: 19
  Hometown: Williams
  State: Arizona
  Component: US ARMY
  Organization: 27th Armrd Inf Div
  Military Occ: Inf
  Grade: Cpl
  Battles and Campaigns: Rhineland Ardennes GO 40 WD 45, Normandy GO 33 WD 45
  Born: 7 May 24
  Deceased: 7 Mar 45

Warren Sam Simpson
  Age: 19
  Hometown: Williams State: Arizona
  Component: US ARMY
  Organization: 27th Armrd Inf Div
  Military Occ: Inf
  Grade: Cpl
  Battles and Campaigns: Rhineland Ardennes GO 40 WD 45, Normandy GO 33 WD 45
  Born: 7 May 24
  Deceased: 7 Mar 45

. . .

"Your suspicions were correct, they were indeed soldiers—corporals—in the army and served in Europe. It looks like they were in the 27th Armored Infantry, which was in Bradley's First Army. Probably landed at Omaha Beach sometime after D-Day but were replacements, like the letters say. Went through Normandy and on to Paris, like the letters say, and then made it into the Battle of the Bulge, which is more correctly called the Ardennes Offensive. But they don't have any citations after that.

"Let me dig a little bit more here."

Colonel Hurley continued typing, pausing, typing, and then shook his head. "I'll keep looking, but...well, let me try...okay. It looks like their unit was captured right after the German army began the Ardennes Offensive. That means they were probably in a prisoner-of-war camp after January 1945.

"Well, this is getting more interesting. Researchers are going to eat this up. The date of death was March 7? They probably died in that camp."

Mogi and Jennifer had been looking closely at the screen and now leaned back in their seats. Jennifer spoke first.

"I think Margaret Simpson believed that she'd found a way to make up for all the time she'd had to deny her sons a real family life. She was rejected by her family, restricted by her job, and had to pretend that her sons didn't exist just so they could survive.

"If she planned the robbery or just helped make it happen, she did it for the love of her boys. Her dreams must have been rock solid to keep her going for nearly two years. And when she found out they had died, everything ended."

Mogi leaned forward. "It looks like the twins stayed together throughout the war. Wyatt wrote fourteen letters, which is like a couple per month for the seven months between June, when they landed in Normandy, and December or January, when they were captured."

"If they did die in a POW camp," Colonel Hurley added, "then the date of their deaths may not be exact. The Graves Registration Unit retrieving their bodies would have interviewed the former prisoners to help pin down a reasonable date, as well as going through any of the German logbooks that might have been available. Oh, and we could..."

He typed for a few minutes more and then sat back in his chair. "They're buried in the Netherlands American Cemetery in Margraten, Netherlands. The date of death is the same—the 7th of March, 1945."

Mogi sat back with a look of satisfaction that quickly shifted to sorrow: "Exactly two months before Margaret Simpson killed herself."

CHAPTER 19

The idea came to her the third time Harold Lennon met her at the park. The first time, the trees were summertime lovely, and he introduced himself to the lovely lady sitting alone on a bench by offering to share his sandwich. He seemed nice, and eager to show himself as important: As senior clerk at the bank, he was a key player in everything that went on.

By their third meeting, he had gotten to describing the details of the various ways that money came into the bank and how it was distributed around town. When he talked about the transfers from the Kansas City bank, she had something close to a vision—all those hundred-dollar bills, stacked on a table and left alone in the vault, waiting to be sorted. If someone were in a certain place at a certain time under the right circumstances, that someone could remake their future.

Over the next few weeks, listening to Harold and asking seemingly innocent questions, Margaret memorized the setup—the delivery routine, the dollar amounts, the 120 layout of the vault, how the bills were handled, who was where when. Harold even gave her a guided tour.

Her vision grew until it was a full-blown cinematic movie in which a poor, separated, victimized family find themselves united and free from the bondage they had always known. She was ready to work out the details.

Margaret played the depot chief like she played Harold.

When business in the dining areas was light, she would dash out with a piece of pie or a cup of freshly brewed coffee for him, making him feel special in the eyes of a pretty woman. Then, as soon as she knew the boys in California were boarding a train headed for Santa Fe, fresh from basic training, and bound for Kansas, she asked one special favor: Two soldiers, sons of a close friend, had sent a wire saying that they were coming through, could she know the time so she could surprise them with gifts?

Getting that information had been more difficult and the timing more critical, but Margaret was convinced that, with initiative, boldness, and courage, she could make up for all those times of abandonment her boys had suffered.

Destiny had laid down a path for her to follow.

Years later, Margaret Simpson now stood in the center of her bedroom, slowly turning in a circle, looking at her few possessions, remembering.

Two months before, the friend who had kept the boys in Williams forwarded the letters from President Roosevelt telling her of their fate: They had died fighting the enemy of the free world.

The boys were never coming back. They had died together as they were born together, and Margaret's dreams died with them.

She decided to die too.

So shall it be. The graves were done, the headstones done, the preparations done. The date she had chosen had arrived, and only the final step was left.

She continued to turn in the center of the room, her hands and arms outstretched, as if sweeping the mist of memories.

The train, the troops, the bank, the money, the bag of clothes, watches, and guns—nothing was sure, and timing was everything. In fact, it had been outlandish to even think that all those events could ever come together perfectly. But she had prayed so hard, so often, that she'd proceeded as if God himself had guaranteed the outcome.

Margaret had told the boys that everything might fall through at the last second, so they had to be prepared to turn around and have lunch if they didn't find the bag.

But everything worked perfectly, from start to finish, as accurate as the pocket watches she had bought for their sixteenth birthdays, the only belongings she could not bring herself to destroy.

She'd almost met them after the deed was done. Almost. It had been a matter of seconds maybe, the bag still warm from Warren's shoulder. They must have jammed the duffel under the dormitory's back step just as she came through the front door.

Seconds. She had missed them by seconds. Just a glimpse, she wished. Just a glimpse would have calmed the longing inside her.

Margaret hustled the bag to her room and reappeared in the Castañeda without missing a beat. That night, she put the clothing, hats, and pistols in another bag and then used the tunnels to get to the steam house, tucking the green cloth bag of money up behind the pipes on the way.

The other bag she tossed into the furnace, whatever remained would never be noticed when the coal ashes were dumped out. She would return for the money once she'd finished preparing its final hiding place.

Enough. So shall it be.

She gave herself one last inspection in the mirror, looking for smudges, dirt, loose threads, uneven hems, wrinkled sleeves, but she was perfect, as every Harvey Girl should be. She left her white apron on the bed.

Margaret made sure the note was plain and obvious on her pillow, then listened at the door. Everyone was asleep, she needed to complete the final step without interruption. She slipped out the front door and quietly closed it behind her.

May 7. Their birthday—the reason she had waited for this day. So many years of loving them fiercely, so few minutes of holding them in her arms. Soon, they would all be together again.

A few minutes later, in the darkness of the rail-yard, she placed her foot on each of the rails to feel for the vibrations telling her the train was coming. When she found the right track, she stood quietly, looking for the light, listening for the whistle, waiting for the moment.

CHAPTER 20

PRESENT DAY

t was Friday, July 28, the day before the Harvey Girl reunion at the Castañeda Hotel. Prompted by their talk with Colonel Hurley on Monday, Mogi and Jennifer used Tuesday afternoon to recheck dates, ages, locations, and other details from their discoveries, to write down their thoughts about Margaret's life in Chinle and Williams, to add in the information on the twins' war years, and to draw a timeline that simplified what happened.

But there were still gaps: Margaret's early life in Chinle, the circumstances of her pregnancy, where her boys lived and who cared for them while she was in Las Vegas, and what she had done with the duffel bag of money and clothes after the robbery.

Everyone would want to know what happened to the money, but Mogi and Jennifer didn't know. They were sure that Margaret, with her boys gone, no longer cared about the money. Maybe she'd destroyed it so no one would benefit from their crime. Maybe she left it untouched. Maybe she had just forgotten to leave any hint for finding it.

On Wednesday, they made hard copies of their account for Sue and Dr. Sanford and then sent the electronic copy to the class members and to the Harvey House Museum historian in Belen.

Dr. Sanford was stunned. The owner of the Castañeda was shocked. It was a remarkable tale, they all agreed, and they praised Jennifer and Mogi for finding the information and filling in so much of the story. The team members emailed congratulations.

But the story they had written and the way they put the facts together were only fascinating theories unless they could find some kind of proof. It was disappointing to Jennifer and irritating to Mogi, but he agreed that they had used a lot of imagination to connect the dots. They had, at least, answered a slew of the questions he had laid out, and he was happier than the week before. But without proof, he and his sister had done no more than provide a good mystery with only a made-up solution.

Mogi thought Gabriel Sanchez was going to be the big winner. He wouldn't have to lie about the information, even if it wasn't enough to prove anything, but he had never been concerned about proving anything anyway.

If he wrote the stories right, he could sell them to a newspaper or magazine and might even gain a better standing in the English department. He might get out of Las Vegas sooner than he'd expected.

Mogi took a deep breath. He and his sister had done all they could do. It was time to get the reunion over with.

———

Representatives from local organizations were busy Friday afternoon, arranging the tables and chairs for the banquet, putting up easels with poster boards of information throughout the hallways, and setting out brochures while the hotel's work crew was giving a final polish to the banisters and vacuuming the entryway.

The assessment team carried the display items from the upstairs room to the tables in the lobby. To illustrate what life was like in the Harvey Girl dorm rooms, the team moved a bunk bed, a mattress, a dresser, a nightstand, a sink with faucets, a lamp, a ceiling light fixture, and an old rug to a corner of the lobby, and then arranged them to simulate a bedroom. Local antique stores contributed authentic Harvey Girl items, including dresses, aprons, shoes, hats, and linens.

With their prized possession now back in hand, Jennifer worked to create the original display she had planned, directing Mogi and Sue to hang the quilt as a backdrop to the footlocker. Not quite getting it right, they left the job for the next morning. They went to

Taco Bell for a late-night snack, then back to the dorm for some well-earned sleep.

By seven the next morning, the three were making their final trips up and down the stairs. The hotel would be opening for tours at nine o'clock.

With just two hours left, hanging the quilt became Mogi's focus. Sue frantically ran out to a hardware store to get a selection of wall hangers. Ultimately, the quilt was hung and the footlocker placed on a short table to allow easy viewing inside while the contents were spread across a larger table next to it. An easel held a large poster with Mogi and Jennifer's story of Margaret Simpson and her boys, the bank robbery was not mentioned.

Photographs and captions were placed next to the items or taped to the table fronts. The prize of the day was Colonel Hurley's bringing enlargements of the Army photographs of Warren and Henry. They were handsome men. Jennifer quickly mounted the pictures on the poster.

Outside, more than a dozen vendors in pickups, vans, and trailers were setting up large folding shelters with tables and chairs and laying out their arts and crafts for sale.

Food vendors were already selling breakfast burritos and honey-covered fry bread. Green chile stew was simmering in large pots and would lead the menus for lunch.

The Castañeda's owner, sweating in a turn-of-the-century Western suit and tall beaver-skin hat, was busy with last-minute preparations, calling crew members to hustle with extension cords, helping to move shelters to their correct spots, and greeting the ladies from the Las Vegas Historical Society, who were dressed in Harvey Girl skirts, blouses, hats, and aprons. They would lead tours and monitor visitors as the crowds wandered around in the expansive hotel.

As nine o'clock struck on the old clock in the lobby, the owner made a grand gesture and opened the front doors, welcoming the surge of people.

Jennifer was still tweaking the exhibit when her brother yielded to the anticipation and excitement and hurried to view the New Mexico History Museum displays, the Las Vegas Historical Museum's photographs, and the information from the Chamber of Commerce about other historic Las Vegas buildings.

The wave of people soon jammed the hotel lobby as everyone slowed to look at the displays. Jennifer found herself giving an ongoing presentation on the building's artifacts and the work of the assessment team. She and the other team members barely had time to breathe as the visitors, fascinated by the artifacts, asked for more and more information.

The official Harvey Girl reunion and festivities were scheduled for eleven. The luncheon—open only to invitees—would be held first, followed by talks and recognition. Each of the honored Harvey Girls was given a corsage to wear and could be seen negotiating the crowded lobby with their escorts, looking at the displays.

Only a few braved the stairs to revisit the rooms they had known so long ago. Small groups of women cried openly as they recognized each other, and many invaded the dining room to find empty tables to sit and chat.

Walking the grounds outside, it seemed to Mogi that half of Las Vegas was wandering the side yards and the courtyard, visiting the booths, hustling into lines at the food vendors, and moving in and out of the hotel. A group of musicians performed on the back porch while children played on the dry fountain.

The Castañeda festivities were far more impressive and interesting than anything produced in Bluff, and Mogi was caught up in the music, the chatter, the noise, and the happiness of the event. Treating himself to a funnel cake with powdered sugar sprinkled on top, he strolled about and finally settled on the side of the courtyard porch.

———

As Mogi sat enjoying the views and the people and the music, a man stood in front of a food booth, keeping himself hidden from Mogi's view. He was a stout and well-muscled, with a beard. He had been watching the young man for some time, and now that Mogi seemed settled, he made his move.

Jack Grimes turned and made his way through the crowd, casually walking back to the front of the building and through the front door. He watched as Jennifer chatted with visitors at the table.

———

As the lobby clock chimed ten o'clock, Mogi wandered back into the hotel. Rows of people two deep still milled in front of the displays. Mogi checked his watch.

There was plenty of time before the luncheon. He looked for his sister but didn't see her. Another team member was behind the table serving as host and talking to visitors. Mogi drifted through the crowd until he was next to the footlocker, appreciating the attention it was getting. It was proving to be the crowd-pleaser that Jennifer had expected.

The newspapers were laid out in fan-fashion, each one folded to show the date and the main headline, a piece of clear Plexiglass had been laid over them. Next to it was a small poster listing some of the interesting things found in the newspapers: the progress of the war, the bank robbery, people being married or celebrating anniversaries, the names and dates of funerals, some quirky items being advertised.

Photocopies of Wyatt's letters were taped to a long display board in front of the counter, and many visitors bent over them to read. People indeed wanted to see what a soldier on the front lines of combat had to say.

The other contents were likewise placed across the table: the Bible, the stack of pay stubs, the ledger page, the clothes, the shoes, the hat. The quilt was still hanging straight, but Mogi wondered if people even noticed it. It hardly seemed personal enough to be connected to the footlocker or to Margaret Simpson.

"Hey, have you seen my sister?" Mogi asked, leaning through the visitors to catch a team member's attention.

"Yeah. She went outside with some guy."

"What guy?"

"I don't know. Some guy with a beard. He was asking a lot of questions about the letters, and then they both left."

CHAPTER 21

Mogi was out the door and off the porch before realizing that he had no idea where he was going. Jack Grimes had Jennifer.

He didn't know where they were, he didn't know what on earth Grimes wanted her for, and he didn't know why—oh, why—she'd be stupid enough to ever leave the building with him.

Sue. He had to find Sue.

Mogi burst back through the front door, impolitely bumping into bodies as he swung around in a circle, wondering where Sue would be, and then headed for the dining room.

She was at a corner table surrounded by other team members.

"Jennifer—have you heard from her?" he asked quickly.

Sue frowned and shrugged her shoulders.

"Grimes has her!" he blurted out. "He was here. He

got her to leave with him, and now she's gone! Have any of you seen my sister?"

The mention of Jack Grimes's name brought nothing from the rest of those seated at the table, but it brought Sue to her feet. "You're kidding! Where'd they go? What does he want?"

"I don't know!" Mogi almost screamed, close to hysterics. HE HAS HER was blaring itself through his body.

It was the most unnerving feeling he'd ever felt.

Sue grabbed him by the arm and led him back through the lobby and out the front door. She said nothing until they had reached the parking lot, away from the crowds.

She pulled her phone from her back pocket. "Okay, get ahold of yourself. I'm going to text her. Tell me everything that happened."

Mogi started pacing back and forth, swinging his arms and punching the air. "It was time to get together for the luncheon. I asked the guy behind the display table, and he said that some guy with a beard had come to the table and asked for her and they'd gone out the door, but I don't know why she would do that unless he was forcing her because she knows better. She knows better than to leave alone with anyone, so she's got to be here somewhere—"

"Okay, settle down," Sue said as she grabbed his arm. "She's in the annex across the street, the same room where we found the footlocker. Grimes must be with her, but at least she answered my text."

It took a second to understand what Sue had said,

but when he did, Mogi pulled away and sprinted past her in a panic.

Idiot! Idiot! Idiot! Why hadn't he texted her and gotten the information himself? Why can't he ever get things right?

He ran. Fast.

He knew that Sue didn't have a key to the building and figured that if Grimes had Jennifer in the back room, he must have picked the lock on the back door, which would now be locked, so Mogi couldn't use it to get in the building.

Mogi launched himself into the piece of plywood over a window opening. He heard Sue scream. He hadn't really thought of what slamming into a big piece of plywood might feel like, but when the board gave way and crashed to one side, he slid onto the muck-covered floor and rolled over before struggling back to his feet. Wow, his shoulder and hip really hurt a lot more than it looks like in the movies, but he had to get to Jennifer.

The door to the back room was open, and Jennifer was rushing out as he started down the hallway. She caught him halfway and wrapped her arms around him, squaring her feet to stop his momentum.

He was shaking hard, and he squirmed in her arms, crying but ready to fight hell itself if it was between him and his sister.

"Hey! Hey!" he heard Jennifer say. She kept her grip around him. "I'm okay. Hey! Look at me! I'm okay! Oh my God! You're bleeding!"

He was. The sharp edges of the plywood had

slashed his arm. Though blood wasn't spurting out, it was running down onto his hands.

He hadn't noticed. He was still shaking, in the grip of terror and exploding energy. Jennifer held him until his heaving chest gradually calmed.

Sue came into the room, having carefully stepped over the window frame and picked her way around the scattered plywood.

"Wow, that was impressive." She turned to Jennifer: "You okay?"

"I'm fine. I've just got to get Mogi settled down here. Do you have any tissues or water or anything? He's bleeding a little."

"A little? I'm surprised he's not wearing most of that plywood."

Gabriel Sanchez came out of the back room. "Here," he said, handing Jennifer a handkerchief.

"You? You're not Jack Grimes," Sue said.

Sanchez gave a little smile and shrugged. "Well, that's at least one thing I don't have to lie about."

Once Mogi had calmed down and she'd wrapped the handkerchief around his arm, Jennifer led everyone into the room. An older man, stoutly built, with a salt-and-pepper beard, was sprawled on the floor. His hands were held together behind his back with a large zip tie. "That's Jack Grimes?" Mogi asked.

Sanchez held up a driver's license. "In the flesh. His license says he's from Trenton, New Jersey."

Mogi looked at his sister. "I thought he took you and I couldn't do anything about it and I didn't know where you were but you answered Sue's text... Wait a minute, how did he end up on the floor?"

She pointed at Sanchez. "My hero, I guess."

Sanchez was still smiling. "I came to the reunion this morning to see if Grimes would show up. When he did, and grabbed your sister by the arm and walked her over here, I came up the other end of the alley and snuck in behind them after he opened the back door. Then I used this on him." Sanchez held up a palm-sized stun gun.

"You did that?" Mogi asked. "Wow. You probably keep that around to use on dastardly criminals."

Sanchez laughed. "Yep. Gotta be ready for people like that."

The man on the floor was groaning now, rolling around the floor. He finally pushed himself into a sitting position. He was trying to stand up when Sanchez went over and waved the stun gun in his face.

"I'd stay down if I were you."

Grimes scooted backward until he was against the wall.

"I didn't do anything. I touched her arm, but that's all. I wasn't going to hurt her. I just wanted to ask her about the letters."

Sanchez waved the stun gun at him again. "On the other hand, let's have another go. I kind of liked watching you drool while you flopped around."

"Okay, okay," Jennifer said, stepping toward Grimes.

"Lay it all out. Who are you, what are you doing

here, and how come you know so much about Margaret Simpson?"

The man looked up at her, squirmed into a better position, and answered. "My grandfather died last year. Before he did, he told me a story of being captured in World War II and being put in a prisoner-of-war camp. He told me he met two brothers there who'd been captured when their unit got surrounded when the Bulge started. They'd been in the camp for two months and looked in bad shape. It was sometime in March because it was still freezing at night and nobody had enough clothes.

"POW camps might have been better than the damn concentration camps, but they were still miserable. My granddad said it was cold and wet, the barracks only had tiny stoves with a few handfuls of coal, and there wasn't any food except for what the Red Cross sent. The camp doctors had no medicine, there was lots of lice, and people were dying by the dozens every week. The guards made everyone stand outside for hours every morning while they took their sweet time with roll call, making the prisoners all sick as hell.

"The brothers had both gotten dysentery, which gives you diarrhea three or four times a day and makes you lose water like a fire hydrant. A couple of days and you turn into a skeleton. My granddad listened to them one night when they started talking, they knew they weren't going to make it. They'd grown up in Arizona without a dad, watching their mom work her fingers to the bone to provide for them. They were twins, see, one always doing what the other one did, and my granddad thought it was amazing that they were born together and were going to die together.

"They kept talking about their mom and how they'd failed her and how she'd give up on life if they didn't make it. Then they started talking about this bank in New Mexico. They'd robbed it while passing through town on a troop train, timing everything with the pocket watches she'd bought them for their sixteenth birthday. Their mom worked in the same town, so they left the money with her and got back on the train. She was going to hide the money until they came back. A couple of days later, they were both dead.

"My grandfather had never talked about the story before—and I'd talked to him plenty about his experiences in the war—but you know how old people can suddenly remember past events really well. Early in the summer, some TV news channel he was watching reported about this old footlocker being found in an abandoned hotel in New Mexico, and it had two pocket watches in it and letters from a soldier written to a waitress in 1943. He figured that they had to be talking about the boys' mother. Her name was Simpson, and he remembered that that was the twins' name.

"I searched online about bank robberies in New Mexico and found a story about one in 1943 that matched the soldiers' story exactly. That cinched it for me. With nobody else knowing that a couple of

GIs had gotten off a troop train to rob a bank and then left the loot with their mom, I figured I had a head start in searching for the money. I just needed somebody to help me."

"That's why you contacted me?" Sanchez asked. "And lied about being a treasure hunter?"

"I'm from New Jersey. What the hell do I know about this dumpy little town in New Mexico? I needed somebody to do the legwork, and you seemed like just the kind of sucker to do it."

"Thanks for that," Sanchez said, rolling his eyes. "But how did you know about the hundred-dollar bills in the Bible?"

"The brothers knew their mother would never spend a dime of the stolen money until they got back, so they told her to take some of the bills, hide them in her Bible, and use the money like it was her own. They didn't want her to be living poor while they were overseas. They figured she deserved better.

"They asked my granddad to go see their mother after the war if they didn't make it. They wanted him to tell her that they loved her and were sorry about dying, but that she should take the money and make a new life for herself. To make sure she'd believe he had met the two of them, they told him to ask her if she'd ever spent the money hidden in the Bible."

"Did the brothers say anything about where she hid the rest of the money?" Mogi asked.

"Shoot, they didn't even know. All they knew was that she'd hold it till they got back."

"Why didn't your granddad find her after the war?" Mogi asked.

Grimes looked at him with mean eyes. "He always meant to but never got to where he could afford it. They weren't the only ones making requests like that. If you'd heard what my granddad told me about living in that POW camp, you wouldn't ask stupid questions. He was barely hanging on, watching men all around him dying, all the deathbed crap people were making up."

"But why did you steal the footlocker?" Jennifer asked.

"And why did you steal the building keys when you're obviously good at picking locks?"

"You young kids, you think you know everything. I grew up in the projects in Trenton. I could pick any lock in the building before I was out of junior high. I stole the keys to put you on the wrong track. Getting into that room upstairs in the hotel was no problem. I was looking for anything that might help, but when I saw the footlocker, I figured it was the most likely place that Mama Simpson would hide her secrets, so I took it."

"But even with the footlocker, you were as stumped as we were," Mogi said, "so you broke into my dorm room looking for more."

"You're a pretty smart kid. When I took everything out of the locker and stuck the stuff up on the wall, the letters were really interesting. They were different. So different, in fact, that I was sure that's where the message was hidden. But I stared at them till I was blue in the face and finally gave up. They were nothing.

"Then you creeps stole the footlocker back and left me high and dry. Time was getting short living in that motel, so I broke into your room, thinking maybe you'd kept something out of the footlocker. When I saw the copies of the letters on the wall and the marks you made all over them, I knew you'd figured out something or were close. I figured the message had to be in the letters and I had just missed it. So I took them.

"I taped your letters up on the walls like you did," he said as he pointed to Mogi's letters on the walls behind him, "looked and looked at them but got nothing. Nothing! I couldn't make out anything more than I did with the originals.

"I thought Sis here might know what you found, so when I saw you outside and her inside, I thought that if I could bring her over here and get her to look at all the marks you'd made on the letters, she'd tell me what you'd figured out."

"Why'd you beat the crap out of me?" Sanchez asked.

"I can't live in a motel forever. I needed to find the money and go home, or at least give up. I thought maybe a little pressure on you might make the others a little more desperate."

CHAPTER 22

Sanchez took charge of introducing Jack Grimes to the local police while Mogi, Sue, and Jennifer went back to the hotel.

They stopped long enough to make a better bandage for Mogi's arm and then slipped into the dining room while the woman from the history museum was finishing her presentation. As they found seats next to the other team members near the back of the room, Dr. Sanford's expression let them know she was not pleased that they'd missed their part of the program.

The Harvey Girls were having a great time. They were clearly honored to be given such recognition, but it was hard for the speakers to present Harvey House history because a chorus of voices would suddenly break in and correct them, or tell some anecdote or story, or share a fun fact, or give the name of a certain young man who'd snuck into the dormitory, or share the fright of having been caught out after curfew by the house mother.

The festivities had already taken forty-five minutes longer than planned.

Finally, the cake was brought out, a last congratulatory speech was given, and the Harvey Girls continued to chat among themselves. All of them. At once. No one got up to leave. It looked like they were going to stay for supper.

Jennifer rose from her chair and moved to the microphone. She used a fork to tap on her water glass, producing a ring that quieted the room.

"If you don't mind," she said, "I have one more thing that needs to be said."

The guests gave her their attention. They could tell this was not part of the planned program.

"I can't let everyone go away without saying something about Margaret Simpson."

The eyes of every Harvey Girl were now focused on Jennifer. They had all passed by the footlocker, looked at its contents, and read the notes that reminded them of Margaret's years at the hotel and her suicide. The letters were also read, and many of the women had comments about their own family's soldiers. None of the presenters had mentioned Margaret.

Jennifer introduced herself and explained what her job had been with the assessment team, adding that she had been living with Margaret Simpson's legacy for most of the summer.

"How many of you knew Margaret?" Jennifer asked.

Every guest raised her hand.

"Uh, really? You all knew Margaret?"

Every head nodded, all smiled, and one woman added, "She was the house mother when we worked at the Castañeda. She ran this place like Patton ran his army!"

There were laughs and grins and many oh-yeses.

"Did you know she had children?" Jennifer asked.

A few women nodded. One lady at a front table called out, "We all had secrets. When the war kept dragging on and so many of us were losing our friends and family, pretty soon everybody got to know everybody else's secrets, and Margaret wanted so much to talk about her twins. She was so proud, and you know, things are different for a mother of twins, don't you think?"

Others nodded.

"When the boys died, it was hard for her. It was only two months or so before the end of the war in Europe. Such a shame. She was devastated. I expect that's why she chose to take her life."

That increased the crowd's attention and made Jennifer bolder about her next question. They might know everything, but it didn't mean that they wanted to talk about it.

"Did you know about her boys and the bank robbery?" Jennifer asked. "This is a part of her story that may seem terrible—and I feel terrible having to tell you—but it will all be in the papers now, and I think it's better that you hear it from me first."

Now there was dead silence in the room. After a few moments, one of the guests stood up. She was elderly and thin, but she stood erect and spoke in a strong voice: "Jennifer, we were all damaged by the war. I'm not sure you can understand or appreciate it, nor do I think I can really explain it. For some of us, the damage was great and impacted the rest of our lives. Others healed and went their own way.

"But we Harvey Girls couldn't do our jobs during the war without losing part of ourselves. We watched a continuous stream of young men come and go in those trains, and we knew that a great many of them would never come back. We knew that every soldier had a mother, a father, sisters, brothers, grandparents. We watched them smile, joke, talk excitedly, and gobble down their food, but every one of us was left with a hole in our hearts when they got back on those trains. It was hard to believe in the sacredness of life anymore, about the supposed safety of family, and especially about the honor that it was supposed to be to die for your country.

"We who were left behind learned to treasure whatever we could, and in the darkest parts of the war, that meant everything. We loved Margaret, we all loved her, and we knew that she loved us, deep down. But there is no love like a mother for her kids, and for her, her twins were the world.

"She suffered more than we knew by having those kids and being their only source for survival. She had been abandoned by her family, by the father of those boys, by her church. She was all those boys had for years and years, but she could not excuse her absence, could not forgive herself for not being there as they grew up. When an opportunity presented itself, she yielded with the greatest hope that it would make her dreams for the family come true.

"She and the boys did something that they should not have done. Not one of us would claim that they were doing right. She was sorry, she really was, but it was done for the love of her children and her desire that they, as a family, could restart their lives. The boys never doubted their mother and followed her without question.

"Most of us were ignorant of the robbery, but toward the end of the war, a few of us became a sort of father-confessor for her, an inner circle of trust. We listened as she wept over what they had done and how she had never anticipated the emotional cost of taking part in such a crime.

"She had to bare her soul. She had been so alone most of her life, so solitary, and she felt so vulnerable. We provided her the safety of confession, and after she was gone, we made a pact to never say a thing. God knows that Margaret Simpson did some wrong things, but we think she made up for them by all the good things she did.

"She raised those boys however she could, just like she raised us. She was our anchor in troubled times when we needed her, and we became the keepers of her memories. She was much more than a house mother. I only hope that I've lived my life well enough to deserve her."

The woman sat down.

Jennifer was already crying, as were most of the guests.

She had planned to say more, but there was no longer a need. She raised her water glass and said, "Let us remember a woman who loved her children as all mothers should love their children."

CHAPTER 23

"Are we still going to make a detour before we get on the highway?" Jennifer asked as she turned out of the dormitory parking lot.

"If we've got enough time," her brother answered.

"I think we've got plenty of time. Since Dr. Sanford was so proud of the reunion and the exhibits that she decided the report would count as the final exam, we'll be back in beautiful Bluff a few days early. I just hope we can find what we're looking for today."

Jennifer turned right instead of left, drove over the bridge into Old Town, went past the plaza, and turned again to the right. The streets got rougher as they led higher up the plateau. She finally pulled into a small parking lot at the Las Vegas Cemetery.

Looking at a guide to the burial plots that she'd found online, they walked to an older part of the cemetery. It took only a few minutes to find what they were looking for.

Margaret Beth Simpson
Jan 6, 1908—May 7, 1945
Harvey Girl and Loving Mother

"According to the historian in Belen," Mogi said, "she bought the plot and paid for the gravestone a couple of weeks before she died, leaving a note specifying that she be buried here. The Fred Harvey Company carried out her wishes and arranged for the funeral. At the burial, they found these." Mogi stepped to the plot next to Margaret's. "She had actually paid for three plots and three gravestones."

A gravestone identical to Margaret's had been placed on the plot. It read:

Henry LeRoy Simpson
Killed in Action, WWII
June 24, 1924—March 7, 1945
Blessings Come From Within

And on the plot next to it, another gravestone read:

Warren Sam Simpson
Killed in Action, WWII
June 24, 1924—March 7, 1945
Blessings Come From Within

"These graves are empty, of course," Mogi said. "Both boys are in the American cemetery in the

Netherlands, as Colonel Hurley told us. Maybe someday we can go see them."

The brother and sister walked over to a bench beneath a tree and sat down. The sun was already hot though it was still early morning, but the shade was cool and the air heavy with the smell of freshly cut grass. Hundreds of trees scattered among the grave markers cast their irregular shadows, and a gentle breeze made the leaves twitch and dance.

They were alone except for a woman in a long black dress on the other side of the cemetery, standing beneath a tree.

"When we were in the Rawlins Building that first time," Jennifer said quietly, "I didn't tell you everything."

Mogi looked at her.

"When you and Sue were in the upstairs rooms and I went downstairs, I wanted to see if I could tell which bedroom had been Margaret's. The house mother would have had a good view of the back door, but she would also have to be close enough to the stairway to hear anyone sneaking up or down. It had to be one of the two rooms at the bottom of the stairs, and as soon as I went into the room on the left, I knew it was hers.

"Going through the door was like passing through a curtain to a different...place. The room felt colder than the others, and—"she swallowed and continued in a quavering voice—"I heard a woman crying. Softly at first, and then increasing until she was sobbing her heart out. I don't remember kneeling, but suddenly, I was on my knees, and I was the one crying."

Mogi was staring at her in amazement as she looked back at him with sadness.

"I think a mother losing a child would shake the foundations of the earth with her grief, and Margaret Simpson had just lost two. At the same time. And in a foreign country, thousands of miles away. She couldn't even bury them properly, these sons who had been, for most of her life, hidden in the shadows because she dared not reveal them. I imagine she hated that they were still in the shadows when they died."

It was a time for silence, and they both allowed themselves the moment.

After a little while, Mogi said, "We need to talk about something else."

"Okay. Whatcha got?"

"Didn't your parents teach you to never go anywhere with strange men?"

"Since I was old enough to understand words."

"Then why did you do it?"

Jennifer took a deep breath and let it out slowly. "He said that he had you, and if I ever wanted to see you again in one piece, I had to go with him."

Mogi's eyes opened wide. After a few beats, he said, "Okay. I can see that. I would have done the same thing. Probably shouldn't tell Mom and Dad, though."

"It was a risky decision, I think," Jennifer said. "Mom and Dad always say that growing up means we'll be responsible for making decisions on our own. I guess that was my time, and I messed it up."

Mogi nodded silently.

"You did a good thing at the reunion," he said. "You got people crying all over the room, that's for sure."

"I had no idea what I was going to say when I stood up. It wasn't right not to talk about Margaret, but I never expected so many people to speak up. What a time it must have been, living among all those different personalities—a bunch of friends who respected each other, who identified with each other, who took care of each other. Can you imagine being in charge of all of them?

"Those women kept her secrets for three-quarters of a century. And what that lady said about the war—I never thought about the damage the war did to those who stayed home."

Mogi nodded. "Colonel Hurley told me he took early retirement and became a teacher because he just couldn't leave his family anymore. His kids had lived through some of their most important years without a father at home. He said he'd missed too much and was still trying to make up for it."

Jennifer nodded. "By the way," she said, "remember Wyatt writing about the engineers who built a steel roadway across a river using big pontoons? Do you wonder if the company was the same one that Grandpa was in, that maybe he helped build the bridge that Wyatt and Doc used to cross the river?"

Mogi smiled. "When I read that, I thought that if Wyatt had lived, maybe he would have met Grandpa at some veterans' reunion and they would have found that, for one small moment in the middle of a great big war, they were only a hundred yards away from each other. Maybe it would have helped them talk about the things veterans never talk about."

The two sat quietly for a while and then wandered around the cemetery, looking at more gravestones. The cemetery, according to the information at the entrance, had been there for more than a hundred fifty years, and held the graves of a number of lawmen as well of men who had tried to kill them.

"Blessings Come From Within," Mogi said as they went from one gravestone to another. "It sounds familiar for some reason, like I've heard it before."

"Sounds like scripture to me."

"I think it sounds like a platitude from some personal success coach."

Jennifer laughed.

Mogi stopped suddenly. "Wait a minute." He closed his eyes for a few moments. "It's on the quilt," he said, opening his eyes wide. "In one of the corners. The letters were stitched on a white cloth using red thread."

"I wish I had your memory."

Jennifer continued strolling past the graves, checking the dates and noting the different names. She turned to point one out to Mogi but found that he had stopped walking. He was standing several yards behind her with his arms raised and crossed above his head.

"Are you okay?" she asked.

He began to laugh. He jumped up and kept on laughing and started dancing a jig, turning around and around.

"We need to go back to the Castañeda!" Mogi shouted.

"What for?"

He caught up to her, still laughing. "We forgot something."

As they made their way to the car, he glanced back.

The woman in black was no longer standing beneath the tree. He didn't see her anywhere.

Mogi was grinning as they drove to the hotel but said nothing. Jennifer parked in a side yard. Sounds of saws buzzing and hammers pounding rang out from the windows. It was the Monday after the reunion weekend, and the demolition crew was busy at work, finally cleared to rip out everything in their path.

"Can we still get into the team room?" Mogi asked as they walked through the front door.

"I think so," Jennifer replied. "They probably didn't even lock it because everything belongs to the owner now. He's going to move it all into a storage trailer once they start remodeling that wing."

The room was indeed open. Mogi scooted his way through the furniture and lifted the footlocker onto the bed. Lifting the lid, he took out the lumpy quilt and laid it on the mattress.

The quilt was heavy and was certainly bigger than the bed frame. It was made from a series of squares, maybe four inches by four inches. The seams between the squares, though done with a sewing machine, were not straight, nor were the squares lined up straight from the top of the quilt to the bottom. And their patterns and colors seemed to be random.

In one corner square was stitched the words, "Blessings Come From Within."

Sliding his hands against the fabric, one on top and the other underneath, Mogi's face lit up with a bright smile.

"You have a pair of scissors?" he asked.

Jennifer found a pair in the box of supplies used for making displays.

Working low on the quilt, Mogi made a cut across a square and then another on a piece of material inside it. Reaching through the cuts, he pulled out some stuffing.

He was clutching a handful of one-hundred-dollar bills.

"Are you kidding me?" Jennifer exclaimed, her eyebrows shooting up as her mouth fell open.

"Feel the quilt," Mogi said. "Run your hands up and down each side. Feel the lumps? Margaret needed a place to hide the money. She had to keep it close but couldn't just put it in a box in the closet or under her bed. So she hid it in plain sight! How clever is that!"

Jennifer didn't believe it—until Mogi cut into another square to prove it. The bills were tucked between two woolen blankets used as layers under the outer cotton layers. Margaret had inserted the folded bills in each of the squares before sewing around them.

"How did you figure it out?" she asked Mogi, who was twirling around, his arms in a victory sign above his head like Sylvester Stallone in *Rocky*.

"It was a lucky guess more than anything," he said, sitting back down and running his fingers inside one of the quilt's sections.

"Putting the phrase *Blessings Come From Within* on a gravestone seemed kind of weird. Why would you put that? I'd have picked some words that sounded more significant, like, *The Greatest Person Ever Born*, or *I'm in God's Arms*, or *Beginning My Journey Back to Dirt*—some quote that really meant something, you know? Anyway, I was looking at the graves of her sons and thinking about the fact that they were both fake. The graves are empty. That made even less sense for such a saying to be on their gravestones.

"That's when I thought the obvious. Aha! She buried the money in the graves! Now the words made sense.

"But I couldn't figure out how she'd pull that off. Somebody at the cemetery would have noticed any hole the gravediggers hadn't dug themselves. And besides, she'd bought the grave sites in 1945—what did she do with the money for two years? What good would it have done to bury any of it at that point? It was just a wrong idea.

"That left me thinking what else the money could have been buried in. That's when I realized that the *within* she'd been talking about referred to the quilt. The proof of her love for the boys—her keeping the money for them all the time they were gone—had to be inside the quilt."

Jennifer gave her brother a round of applause.

"Are we going to tell anybody or just tuck it away in our backpacks?" she said with a smile, fanning the hundred-dollar bills out on the mattress. "I could really use a new car."

Mogi laughed. "Once I get the Nobel Prize in Stockroomism, we'll have enough money to make this look like small potatoes. I vote that we surprise Dr. Sanford, leave her to fight the hotel owner and the bank for it, and you and I make it to Santa Fe in time for enchiladas at Tomasita's, that restaurant next to the train station."

"Works for me," Jennifer said as she folded the quilt, treating it with much more care than she ever had before.

———

Life back in Bluff seemed unremarkable until Jennifer received a package in December from Dr. Sanford. Inside, she found two copies of a newly published book, one for her and one for Mogi.

"Well, how about that?" she said as she passed her brother his copy. It was a small paperback titled *Blessings Come From Within: A Legend of Love, Robbery, and War*, by Gabriel Sanchez. The text on the back cover described it as an authentic account of a New Mexico legend that took decades to solve.

Mogi laughed, paging through the book: "I hope he didn't have to lie too much."

IF YOU LIKED THIS, YOU MIGHT LIKE

TWO THOUSAND GRUELING MILES: THE COMPLETE YA WESTERN SERIES

Two Thousand Grueling Miles: The Complete YA Western Series is a true family adventure tale full of can't put it down action!

Two Thousand Grueling Miles: Thrust into the role of family protector, young Jake Zane faces the ultimate test of survival and resilience on the unforgiving Oregon Trail. With a massive mute escaped slave as his ally, Jake must navigate 2,000 miles of harsh terrain, battling wild animals, severe weather, and threats from both settlers and natives. Together with his mother and sisters, Jake's journey is a testament to the enduring human spirit and the bonds of family.

Rugged Trails: With his fields ravaged by locusts, Jake takes a perilous job as a wagon and mule train guard, tasked with transporting precious cargo across treacherous paths. Facing hostile terrain, inclement weather, and dangerous encounters with both wildlife and outlaws, Jake must ensure the safe passage of the train to secure a future for his family.

Stormy Seas: Upon reaching San Francisco, Jake Zane finds himself entangled with the notorious Sydney Duck gang. With the support of his friend, Lord Stanley-Smyth, Jake embarks on a new adventure aboard a coastal lumber schooner and later a freighter bound for the Sandwich Islands. In this coming-of-age journey, Jake learns the harsh realities of life at sea and the treacherous world of gold-seeking adventurers.

The Piccadilly: Tasked with transforming the infamous Bucket of Blood saloon into The Piccadilly, Jake Zane navigates the dangerous underworld of San Francisco. Under the mentorship of Lord Stanley-Smyth, Jake encounters gamblers, city cops, Chinese tong soldiers, and intriguing soiled doves. In this gripping conclusion, Jake's loyalty is tested as he balances the demands of his employer and the complex dynamics of a city teeming with ambition and peril.

Two Thousand Grueling Miles: The Complete YA Western Series is a riveting young adult western series that captures the heart of American pioneering spirit. Join Jake on his epic journey of survival, courage, and adventure. Dive in today and experience the thrill of the untamed West!

AVAILABLE NOW

ABOUT THE AUTHOR

New Mexico-based **Donald Willerton** is the author of *Death in the Tallgrass*, the winner of the Western Writers of America 2024 SPUR Award for Western Historical Fiction, a finalist in the 2024 American Fiction Awards, and a finalist in the 2024 Storytrade Book Awards. He has written a ten-book Middle Grade/Young Adult mystery series located in the Southwest, two contemporary thrillers, and a fictional World War II adventure novel.

To finance his writing, he used his degrees in physics and computer science as a scientist, manager, and computer specialist, but has always let his curiosity, imagination, and passion for history keep his head aligned with his heart.